A Magic Christmas

Annie Seaton

The Enchanted Village: 1

ISBN 978-1-7643549-5-0

Dedication

*To all my dear readers, wishing you a magical
Christmas.*

A MAGIC CHRISTMAS

ANNIE SEATON

Annie Seaton lives near the beach on the mid-north coast of New South Wales. Her career and studies spanned the education sector, including working as an academic research librarian, a high school principal, and a university tutor until she took early retirement and fulfilled her lifelong dream of a full-time writing career.

Each winter, Annie and her husband leave the beach to roam the remote areas of Australia for story ideas and research. She is passionate about preserving the beauty of the Australian landscape and respecting the traditional ownership of the land. For those readers who cannot experience this journey personally, Annie seeks to portray the natural beauty of the Australian environment—its spiritual locations, stunning landscapes and unique wildlife.

Readers can contact Annie through her website, annieseaton.net, or find her on Facebook and Instagram. To stay up to date with her new releases, subscribe to her newsletter on the home page of her website: Book 2 of the Enchanted Village will be available on her store in early 2026.

http://annieseaton.net

A MAGIC CHRISTMAS

Prologue

Rain misted the London pavement, softening the late afternoon glow of the streetlights until the world looked half-dream, half-memory. Dimity Armstrong moved quickly down past the dark buildings, sidestepping puddles and a steady stream of people under umbrellas. She was late—unforgivably late—for her four p.m. meeting with Lindsay Lyndhurst, her publisher at Moongate Books.

Her phone buzzed in her coat pocket. She slipped beneath the awning of a bookshop, rain dripping down her cheeks as she fumbled for her phone. Great, now she'd look like a drowned rat. But she guessed that people who lived in this country were used to that look. It was a different sort of rain from what she was used to on the Atherton Tablelands: the constant rain was persistent and fine, a damp, cold blanket unlike the tropical downpours back home.

Dimity's breath caught when she saw Lila's name on the screen—her agent. Even now, she had to pinch herself at the thought of having an agent. Her first self-published series had been such a success, in both print and eBook, that she had fielded offers from publishers in the United States and the United Kingdom before finally deciding she needed someone to represent her.

Who would have ever imagined that bookish Dimity Armstrong from Yungaburra, a tiny town in far north Queensland—more Jane Eyre than Jo March—would ever find herself in London, meeting with her publisher and reading text messages from her literary agent?

After reading the text, she blinked, read it again and then held her breath so long that tiny lights burst at the edge of her vision, the world narrowing to the glow of her screen.

Netflix interested in Shadowlands. Potential 6-fig deal. Call after Lindsay meeting. Don't tell her yet! L x

Dimity dragged in a deep breath; a Netflix adaptation would change everything—she would have made it to a level that she hadn't dreamed of in her wildest dreams. All she'd wanted to do was sell enough books to support herself while she kept writing. Maybe Mum would stop asking when she was going to get a "real job".

A shiver ran through her; more from elation than from the cold rain soaking trickling beneath the collar of her coat.

Calm down, she told herself. Wait until you talk to Lila, and read the fine print.

She still wasn't sure how her romantasy about enchanted doorways and troublesome princes had ended up being compared to The Magic Faraway Tree and Game of Thrones. She suspected neither Enid Blyton nor George R. R. Martin would approve. She clutched her phone in disbelief, reading the message one last time to make sure it really was from Lila.

She glanced at the time before slipping the phone into her coat pocket; not only was she sopping wet, she was now five minutes late. The publishing house was just around the corner and up a short flight of stone steps. Maybe her arrival could be seen as fashionably late.

Dimity ran from beneath the awning into the rain, her heart thudding as fast as her thoughts as she turned into St Martin's Lane. The prospect of seeing her enchanted forests and feuding kingdoms on screen sent a rush of cold adrenaline and white-hot excitement surging through her veins.

Calm down, she told herself again.

Ahead, the Georgian building that housed

Moongate Books came into view, its pale stone darkened by the constant moisture. She took a steadying breath and headed for the steps.

With her focus on Lila's news and not on the steps, Dimity misjudged the first one. Her low heel skidded on the wet stone, a sharp scrape swallowed by the traffic noise. The world tilted; cold air rushed past her face as she floundered—then the rain and traffic sounds merged into a single, rushing torrent that washed away all other thought as she tried to regain her balance—then the back of her head met the edge of the step with a dull, cracking thud that sent white light bursting behind her eyes. The world went grey, then black.

'Miss? Miss, can you hear me?'

Unfamiliar voices swirled around her, blurring together as she tried to open her eyes. Rain on her face. The metallic taste of blood where she'd bitten her tongue as she fell.

'Don't move her! Possible neck injury.'

'I'm calling an ambulance.'

'Her pupils are uneven.'

Dimity tried to speak, to tell them she was okay, just a bit rattled, but her mouth wouldn't cooperate. The darkness deepened, swallowing the noise and the cold.

Chapter One

A steady beeping drifted through the fog, slow and rhythmic, pulling Dimity awake. A sharp tang stung her nose, and crisp fabric brushed against her fingers as she flexed them. Her mouth was dry, her head heavy and dull, as if the world had shifted a few inches to the left when she'd fallen.

Oh, crumbs, I have to get to the meeting. I can't be late.

She tried to push herself up, but gentle hands held her down. Why was the footpath so soft, and what was that strong smell?

'I have to go and see Lindsay,' she managed to croak out. 'I can't be late.'

'Ms Armstrong? Can you hear me? Squeeze my hand if you can hear me.'

Dimity felt pressure against her palm and instinctively squeezed back.

'Good, that's good. I'm Dr Hughes. You're at University College Hospital. An ambulance brought you here after you slipped in the rain. You've sustained a head injury.'

Dimity tried to open her eyes. Something was

wrong. She lifted a hand to her face, fingertips brushing against coarse fabric and the edge of tape—a bandage wrapped around her head, covering the wound at the back. Her eyelids were open—she could feel them move—but she couldn't see anything, only a solid wall of black where light should have been. 'Why can't I see? Can you turn the light on, please?' The words scraped out of her throat.

Her hand moved higher, searching for something covering her eyes, but there was nothing. Just the bandage around her head. The darkness wasn't from a covering—it was her eyes; she couldn't see a thing. She blinked a couple of times and then closed her eyes and opened them again.

'What's wrong? Why is it dark?'

A pause.

'Dimity,' Dr Hughes said gently. She could hear him moving closer, the quiet scrape of a chair. 'You've had a nasty fall. You hit your head quite hard. We need you to stay calm, all right?'

'But I can't—' Her voice broke. 'I can't see.'

'I know,' he said softly, the measured tone of someone trying not to alarm her. 'It's likely swelling or bruising around the optic nerves.

We'll run more tests, but for now, I need you to rest. Panic will only make it worse.'

His words reached her, but their meaning slipped away beneath the fear tightening her chest. Swelling . . . bruising . . . more tests. She gripped the edge of the sheet, fingers clenched, fighting the urge to tear away the bandage on her head, to be able to see something—anything. The black behind her eyes wasn't just dark; it was total. It reminded her of the time when she'd hidden in Mum's wardrobe during a childhood game of hide and seek; she had hated the dark ever since and still slept with a night light each night. Her throat tightened, breath catching somewhere between a sob and a gasp. *What if the light didn't come back?*

'Dimity,' Dr Hughes said again, his voice closer now, steady and low. 'You're safe. You're not alone. We've got you on oxygen and fluids. I need you to stay calm. Just breathe for me, all right?'

She heard the soft click of a monitor button, the rustle of his coat as he adjusted something near her arm. His tone never wavered, measured and calm against the chaos churning through her.

'It's frightening, I know.' His voice was soft.

'But fear will only make your body work harder. Focus on my voice. You're doing fine. Think about your breathing—inhale, exhale, slow, steady.'

Panic tore through her chest, and her pulse thudded in her throat, too fast, too loud; every breath came shallow, uneven. The bandage around her head felt tighter now, pressing against her skin, the darkness pulsing behind her eyelids with every heartbeat. She couldn't stop her hands from shaking.

I want to wake up. It's a dream.

'Dimity.' The doctor's voice cut through her panic. 'You're safe here. We're monitoring everything. You're not by yourself.'

His words reached her through the roar in her ears, and she clung to them, counting the seconds between each inhale and exhale until the trembling in her hands began to ease.

##

Over the next day, between periods of rest, Dimity underwent a series of tests. CT scans and MRIs confirmed that her eyes worked perfectly; the fall had injured the part of her brain responsible for making sense of what they saw. In the afternoon, she was fully awake and calm enough to absorb what Dr Hughes was saying.

'You've suffered trauma to your occipital cortex—the area of the brain that processes visual signals—and as a result, you have something called cortical blindness.'

'Blindness?' The word didn't sound real— she couldn't process it—but her body reacted anyway, a cold rush through her veins. 'You mean I'm blind?'

'The condition is often temporary with this type of injury. When you hit your head on the steps, you sustained an injury to the part of your brain that translates what your eyes capture into images. The eyes still work, but the brain can't make sense of what they see,' Dr Hughes said, his tone steady and reassuring. 'Right now, the swelling is interfering with how your brain processes what your eyes see. But I want you to hear this clearly—nine times out of ten, vision returns as the brain heals. I'm confident you'll be one of them.'

Dr Hughes left her as the tea trolley arrived. Dimity was becoming very used to processing the world from the sounds around her.

'A cup of tea, love?' a kind voice asked.

'Yes, please.'

'You be careful.' The woman took her hand and guided it to the polystyrene cup. 'I've pulled the tray up close to you so that you can put the cup down in between sips.'

'Thank you. Can you put my phone on the tray, please? I think it's on the table next to the bed.'

'There you go, love.'

Dimity managed to drink her tea without disaster, and when she put the cup down, she reached for the phone, hoping it still had a charge.

'Hey Siri, call Lila.' Relief filled her when the call rang and then the call connected.

'Dimity! Where in the flamin' hell have you been? I was about to send a search party out. Lindsay rang, looking for you too. Did I scare the living daylights out of you with the Netflix message? Marcus said I should have told you face-to-face.'

'Lila.' Dimity cleared her throat and took a deep breath. 'I had a bit of an accident on the way to see Lindsay. I'm in the University College Hospital.'

'Oh, love, what happened? Are you okay?'

'I had a bit of a fall on the steps at Moongate,

and they brought me here. I've had all sorts of tests, and I'm fine, but I need to see you. Can you come in?'

'I'm on my way.'

As she lay there waiting for Lila, the day nurse came into the ward.

'Dimity, are you up to a visitor? There is a Miss Braithwaite here to see you, and she has a beautiful bunch of flowers for you.'

Dimity frowned for a moment and then remembered that was the name of Lindsay's PA. 'Yes, that's fine.'

Footsteps, obviously high heels, clicked on the floor.

'Oh Dimity, you poor thing, how are you feeling? We were so upset when Lila called and told us it was you who was taken away in the ambulance yesterday afternoon.'

'I'm recovering, thank you, Celia.' Dimity touched the bandage covering her eyes. When the nurse had changed the dressing earlier, Dimity had asked her to put it over her eyes too. It made the dark more bearable when her eyes were covered. She had asked Dr Hughes that no one apart from the medical staff would be told she had lost her sight.

'I'll be glad when this comes off, though.' She wasn't ready for the pity, the careful voices, the inevitable oh, you poor thing. And Dr Hughes had said her sight would likely return—so why make it real, why risk word spreading to Moongate or Netflix before she had a chance to prove she could still deliver?

'Lindsay sent you these flowers,' Celia said, setting the vase beside the bed. 'She asked me to tell you she'll reschedule your appointment as soon as you're up to it.'

'Thank you,' Dimity said. 'They smell beautiful.'

It startled her, how much sharper everything seemed—the fragrance of the flowers, the scrape of a chair leg, the warmth of sunlight across her hands. With her sight gone, the smallest details seemed enhanced.

Not long after Celia left, Dimity heard the soft thud of footsteps in the corridor, the quick snap of an umbrella closing, and Lila's voice—brisk, familiar, already mid-sentence before she reached the bed.

'What's the go with the bandage? I called Lindsay to explain why you didn't show for the meeting.'

'I'll tell you in a minute. What did she say about me not turning up? She's already sent flowers.'

'That's because you are her number one author at the moment, and that's even without her knowing about the Netflix offer. You're hot, babe.' Lila said, shaking the rain from her coat. Droplets of water landed on Dimity's hand, and then she heard the soft thud of a bag landing on the chair and the scrape of metal legs across the floor. 'She's worried about you being in the hospital, love. And so am I. Now tell me why your head is bandaged. Have you got a concussion? You should have called me last night.'

'Sort of. A bit worse than that.' Dimity told Lila everything that had happened and what Dr Hughes had said.

'Oh my God, and you've been dealing with this by yourself for twenty-four hours?' Warm hands gripped Dimity's, and the sweet floral scent of Lila's signature perfume washed over Dimity.

'It's okay. I was a bit out of it until lunchtime today. And I don't want anyone to know.'

'Have you rung home? Does your Mum

know?'

'No. Look, Lila. I'm okay. Just a slight hiccup with my sight, but it won't last long.'

'We'd better bloody hope not. Netflix want a signature this week. I've looked at the contract, and Marcus has given it a second look, and it's bloody amazing.'

'Tell me.'

'Okay, it's a good thing you're sitting down.'

Dimity shook her head. 'Why?'

Lila held her hands even tighter. 'The initial option fee they offered you is a quarter of a million.'

'What? Did you say a quarter of a million? Dollars?'

'Yes, and US dollars. And that's just the upfront development fee. The purchase price they've offered you is 2.5 million.'

'Say that again,' she whispered, her voice rough, barely audible over the sudden, high-pitched whine that had flooded her inner ear.

'2.5 million.' Lila's voice was almost reverent.

To anchor herself to reality—to prove she wasn't adrift in some opiate-induced delusion—Dimity slowly stretched her right leg, feeling for something solid. Her foot reached the cold, hard steel of the bed frame, a rough, undeniable object in her dark world.

'Oh my God, I don't think I've had an accident. I think I'm in a long, vivid dream.'

'No, this is real. It's all true. You've made it big, babe. There are also additional book rights. You'll receive a producer fee and credit if you want it as an executive producer. You're going to get five percent of net profits, and that's just the beginning.' Lila lifted Dimity's hand to her face. 'Can you feel my tears, Dims? As well as being amazing for you, our fifteen percent will make such a difference to Marcus and I.'

Dimity struggled to speak. 'You're the ones who have done all this for me. You deserve it.'

There was silence for a while as Dimity tried to process what this meant. Finally, she spoke. 'What about Lindsay? Will she get a share?'

'Not of the Netflix deal. It's a shame we signed with Moongate, now that you have the Netflix offer. Your book sales will ride on the back of that, and Moongate will get most of it.' Lila was quiet for a moment, her voice lower when she continued. 'For the time being, we'll work with Lindsay, but we'll probably publish independently once we sign the deal with Netflix.'

'I have to finish the book first,' Dimity said quietly. 'And can we even go independent? I've signed a contract with Moongate.'

'We can, but at this point we'll promise delivery, but the Netflix deal stays between you and me until the contract's signed. Not a word to anyone. I'm pleased we took the screen rights out of your contract.'

'I'm pleased you did too. I had no idea there was any chance of that.'

'You undervalue your work, love.'

'But I still worry, it's not a very nice thing to do when Moongate took me on. I feel bad.'

Lila shook her head. 'Dimity, you are a commodity to Moongate; it's not a friendship. And that's why you have me. I do what's best for my client.'

Dimity nodded, and even that left her drained. A wave of tiredness rolled over her, heavy as the fog in her head. There was too much to think about.

Lila caught it straight away. 'Look, love, you sound exhausted. How about I give you five minutes to process all this? I'll go and find us a proper coffee instead of the hospital sludge, and then we'll work out a solution, hey?'

'Thank you,' Dimity murmured, her voice barely above a whisper.

Lila's heels clicked down the corridor, fading beneath the hum of the ward—the rattle of a trolley, the muted call of a nurse, a door swinging shut. For the first time since waking up in the hospital, the fragility of everything she'd built registered. Not just the darkness, but everything it was taking with it—the Netflix deal, her career momentum, the confidence that had been building since she signed with Lila and Marcus. All of it balanced on a manuscript she couldn't finish because she couldn't see, characters trapped mid-battle in a story only she could tell. Her throat tightened, and she pressed her lips together, refusing to let the tears come. Not yet. There had to be a solution.

Moments later, Lila was back, the rich scent of coffee filling the room before her voice did.

'I've put two sugars in it for you,' she said, setting the cup on the tray. Then her tone hardened—full of that unmistakable Lila savvy. 'Now listen to me. There is no way we're letting this deal slip through our fingers. Your story's gold dust, Dimity—and I'll make damned sure it gets to that screen, even if I have to drag it there myself.'

'Lindsay wants it by the end of December. How close are you to finishing it?'

'Not that close.'

'She's got everything booked for release by Easter. Editors, cover designers, publicists and tour dates for you. She knows how well this book is going to sell. You thought your first four self-published books did well. Wait until you see what happens now. The world is waiting for book five.'

'I can't do it, Lila. The first draft is only three-quarters done. My warrior princess is still staring down the Shadow King—and I can't exactly keep going when I can't see. And even if I could, that is rushing the release date. It doesn't leave enough time for proper editing.'

She pulled the chair close again, the legs scraping lightly on the floor. 'You can make that deadline, with help. And it's not only for Moongate's deadline, Netflix want a date too. One that's not too far away. I'd like you to aim for the end of December. We need to nut out a solution to get this book finished.'

Once Dimity accepted that Lila was serious, they tossed around ideas for a few minutes,

Lila firing off suggestions. 'A ghost writer, maybe? Someone to take your notes and finish—

'

'No,' Dimity cut in, sharper than she meant to be. 'Absolutely not. I can't hand over my characters to someone else. And I will probably have my vision back soon, anyway. Dr Hughes is very hopeful.'

'All right, all right,' Lila said, unfazed. 'What about someone to read back what you've written—keep you on track, let your thoughts take over. I mean, you do know what's going to happen next, don't you?'

This time, Dimity smiled. 'Lila, how well do you know me?'

'Right, that was a stupid thing to say. Of course you don't. You're a "pantser".'

'I prefer the term "organic writer".'

'And your stories shine from that,' Lila said quickly.

Dimity nodded. It had taken her a long time to believe it, but she knew now that her stories were special—that they belonged on the shelves beside the writers she'd once admired from afar.

'They do.' But her words were buried in a yawn she couldn't hold back.

Lila's tone softened immediately. 'How about we give it some space, love?'

She leaned down and kissed Dimity's cheek—quick, affectionate, businesslike. For a moment, the human contact settled her—the faint trace of perfume, the warmth of skin, the rustle of fabric close to her ear—small, ordinary things that connected her to reality.

'Something will happen,' Lila said softly, straightening. 'It always does. And I'm going to let you get some rest. Tomorrow you'll be fresh, and a solution will come to us both. Sweet dreams, love. We both know that this is a minor glitch, and you'll be back to normal before we know it.' Lila's voice broke as she spoke, and Dimity knew she was only saying that to make her feel better.

She heard the gentle scrape of the chair moving away to the corner, the rustle of Lila's bag, then the firm click of her heels retreating down the corridor. A door shut, leaving behind the fading trace of coffee and rain—but a faint, stubborn thread of hope remained.

Lying back against the pillow, Dimity tried

her best to hold onto that hope.

Something will happen, Lila had said. Dimity wanted to believe her. She wanted to believe in everything again—the story, the deal, her sight. She turned towards the whisper of the machine at her bedside and let the thought drift with her into sleep.

Chapter Two

Her sleep was restless. Dimity jerked awake, her mind circling back—deadlines, contracts, Moongate, the Netflix deal, the chapters, and the likelihood of the chance slipping through her fingers. But beneath it all lay the deeper terror: the thought of never seeing again. Never writing again. Never being the woman she was learning to be—the one who'd finally started to believe in her own voice, one who'd earned the right to stand beside the writers she'd once admired.

In the quiet hours, when the ward settled, that remaining one chance in ten of permanent blindness that Dr Hughes had spoken about loomed larger than everything else. It threaded through her thoughts, wrapping around her fragility until she could almost feel it tightening, daring her to let go. She turned her face towards the faint hum of the machines, listening, counting, holding on—because as long as she could hear them, she knew she was still here, still fighting.

When morning came, it was the same sound that woke her—the rhythmic hum of the machines, steady and sure. And with it came determination. She couldn't write in London, surrounded by noise and pity and people who meant well but couldn't understand. She needed somewhere familiar, somewhere she could navigate from memory alone. Somewhere, her imagination had always felt at home.

Lila arrived early; her clicking heels and perfume announcing her presence.

'Is my face clean?' Dimity asked.

'Clean and beautiful. You've got your rosy cheeks back this morning. Marcus sends his love.'

'I was worried I had porridge on my face.'

'Well, you haven't, and it's good to see your eyes uncovered too.'

'I asked the nurse to take the bandage off. I don't need it.'

'You're much brighter today.' The chair legs dragged across the floor, and then Lila sat beside the bed.

'You were right, Lila. Something happened. I know what we'll do.'

'That's great. You even sound brighter today. Tell me.'

'I have a cottage I can go to. I can navigate it

from memory. It's quiet there, away from the noise. I could focus.'

There was a pause, long enough for Dimity to hear the faint rustle of Lila's sleeve as she leaned closer, and the interest in her voice. 'Where?'

'The Cotswolds. My great aunt left it to me a while back.'

'You can't just go off on your own, love,' Lila said finally, her voice softer than usual. 'You've been in the hospital. What if something happens? What if you fall? You can't even make a cup of tea without seeing the kettle.'

'I'll manage,' Dimity said quietly.

'Manage?' Lila gave a short, incredulous laugh. 'You make it sound like popping down to the corner shop. We'll need to hire a carer, or at least someone to check on you regularly.'

Dimity shook her head. 'I don't need someone hovering. I just need space. Familiar space. Somewhere I can think. Fire my imagination again. It's in there, Lila. I can feel it.'

For a moment, Lila said nothing. The chair squeaked, and Dimity could hear her pacing, the tap of her heels on the linoleum. Then came a deep sigh—one that signalled she'd given in.

'You're a bloody stubborn woman,' Lila said. 'Alright. The cottage it is. But I'm coming down with you to get you settled, and that's non-negotiable.'

Dimity smiled, relief and gratitude catching in her throat. 'Thank you, Lila.'

'Don't thank me yet, love,' Lila said briskly. 'Wait until you've survived the car ride with me behind the wheel.'

##

Five days after her fall, Dr Hughes returned for what he called "a follow-up discussion"—a more detailed conversation now that the initial shock had worn off and Dimity could properly absorb what he was telling her. 'The good news is the swelling is reducing quickly,' he began. 'And you're experiencing those occasional flashes of light, which suggests some neural pathways are beginning to function again.'

'But?' Dimity prompted. She'd already learned to recognise the careful pause that came before less comforting news.

'But I need to be honest about the timeline. Recovery is highly unpredictable. Some patients regain full vision within days. Others take weeks or months.'

The unspoken words hung between them. She might never see again.

'Most likely, you'll experience gradual improvement—but the timeline is impossible to predict.'

Dimity turned her face towards where she knew the window must be. She'd grown used to the warmth of morning sunshine on that side of the bed. Even though she could feel the warmth of the sunshine, all she saw was darkness—thick and unbroken, pierced only by the occasional flicker of light, like distant fireflies.

'So, what now?'

'Neurological rehabilitation and regular monitoring,' Dr Hughes said, his tone softening. 'And practical adaptation whilst we wait for improvement. You'll need to learn some new skills. Patience is essential.'

Patience. Her fingers flexed, knuckles aching. She could live with temporary blindness, that her sight would return once the swelling subsided—nine out of ten, he'd said. But the unspoken possibility terrified her. What if she was the one? What if the light never came back?

Her chest tightened, her breath catching in

short, shallow bursts. The steady beep of the monitor seemed louder now as she pressed her palms flat against the sheets, needing something real beneath her hands, something solid. Slowly, she pushed the fear aside, focusing instead on those hopeful, faint flashes that flared behind her eyelids. Proof, she told herself, that her brain was trying—that somewhere inside, the world was still there, waiting to be seen again.

Her sight would return.

Chapter Three

A week after her fall, Dimity left the hospital with a white cane she was still learning to use, a bag full of adaptive devices, and a brain that stubbornly refused to process the world beyond brief flashes and shifting shadows. She had a follow-up appointment scheduled with Dr Hughes in another two weeks.

'Remember, recovery isn't a straight line,' he'd said as she prepared to leave. 'Rest when you need to, challenge yourself when you can, and don't lose faith in those flashes. They mean your brain is trying hard—and that's exactly what we want.'

'The cottage,' she said to Lila as they drove out of London. 'It's the answer. It always has been.'

'That's a strange thing to say.'

Aunt Bea always called it her magic cottage. She was a bit of a character.'

Lila laughed. 'I can't wait. Not haunted, is it?'

'No, just special.'

There had always been something about the cottage—how it seemed to breathe with Dimity's moods. She'd spent a year there with her aunt when she first moved to England.

When she was sad, the air felt still, the clock ticking louder. When she was writing, the floorboards settled and the wind softened, as if the house itself was listening. Her best scenes had always come from there. More than once, she'd woken in the small hours with whole paragraphs forming clearly in her mind—voices, settings, scenes as vivid as dreams. Bea used to laugh and say, "It's the house talking to you, love. You just know how to listen.'

She would listen to the house; whether it meant the answer to her manuscript or to her vision, Dimity didn't know yet. But she needed to trust—and the cottage had never failed her when Bea was alive.

Traffic pulsed around them as they left the city, a constant hum beneath the tyres. Without sight, the world came to her in snatches—the coolness of the wind through the open window, the scent of wet bitumen and diesel, the faint click as Lila adjusted the map on the GPS.

Each sound created its own image in her

mind: the echo of a horn somewhere far ahead, the whoosh of another car passing close, the blinker clicking, marking time. The steady motion soothed her at first, until a sudden brightness behind her eyelids reminded her of what she couldn't see. Her heart thudded; that was the first time brightness had appeared. She opened her eyes slowly and lifted her sunglasses.

Her mood plunged. Still darkness.

'We're nearly clear of the city,' Lila said, her voice a bright thread in the noise. 'You'll smell the countryside soon enough, love.'

Dimity smiled faintly. She could already sense it—the air thinning, carrying the scent of open fields and rain-soaked grass. Somewhere ahead lay Bea's cottage, with its uneven flagstones and the faint lavender scent that pervaded each room.

The thought steadied her. For the first time since the fall, anticipation pushed the fear away. She leaned her head against the window, following the hum of the road, and let memory guide her towards the only place that had ever truly felt like home.

She had finally called home yesterday afternoon. Mum had wanted to jump straight on a plane, but Dimity had handed the phone to Dr Hughes to explain the situation—that she was recovering, that she needed rest, not commotion. She'd convinced her mother to stay home, but Mum's voice had held worry, and she'd even blamed Dimity's writing as the cause of the accident.

'If you hadn't been going to the publisher, it wouldn't have happened. And then the reminders that this writing nonsense had never been a safe career. You should have stayed home and taken that real job. Dimity had managed to cope through the tirade, and she could sense sympathy in Dr Hughes' voice as he answered her parents' questions.

She reminded herself to be grateful for the love behind the scolding, even as the words sank deep.

A real job.

The journey blurred into a rhythm of sound and motion until Lila turned off the motorway, and the hum of the road gave way to quiet. The window glass was cold beneath her fingers, even with the air conditioning on.

The car slowed as it turned onto gravel, wheels crunching over stones slippery with dew.

Dimity rolled down her window slightly, inhaling the distinctive scent of the Cotswolds in late autumn—woodsmoke from cottage chimneys and the crisp bite of coming snow.

'We're nearly there,' Lila said from the driver's seat. 'The village looks like a Christmas card already. Lights strung across the high street, wreaths on every door. That bakery you love has pine garlands around the windows.'

Dimity smiled, constructing the scene in her mind from Lila's description and her own memories. The village of Lower Thistlewick had changed little in the nearly two decades she'd been visiting. She had never forgotten her first visit with Mum when she was six years old. It was a magical place. The honey-coloured stone buildings, narrow lanes, and twelfth-century church were as familiar to her as her own reflection—even if it was a reflection she could no longer see.

'There it is,' Lila said warmly. 'Still as lovely as when Marcus and I came for our first meeting with you. I'd forgotten how enchanting Pippin's Nook is. Do you know where the name came from?'

'There's an apple orchard behind the high

stone wall at the back of the garden.'

'Oh, how lovely. You must show me before I leave.'

The car bounced gently along the final stretch of path leading to the cottage. When they stopped, Dimity sat motionless, suddenly overwhelmed by what she was attempting.

Living alone, blind, in a cottage that, whilst familiar, was still filled with potential hazards.

'We can still change plans,' Lila said gently, picking up on her tension. 'My offer to stay stands, or you could come to ours.'

Dimity shook her head firmly. 'No, I need to do this. I need the cottage, and I need to prove to myself that I'm not helpless.'

Just in case, she thought to herself.

The handbrake clicked, the car door opened, and the soft, rhythmic cooing of a wood pigeon drifted across the garden.

Dimity drew in a breath. The air carried the damp, earthy scent of fallen leaves and cooling soil, mingled with the faint sweetness of late roses clinging to the stone wall. Somewhere, a bonfire smouldered — wood smoke curling through the crisp November air, laced with the tang of apples from the orchard beyond. It was a scent she remembered from her childhood visits, and that wonderful, long year with Bea before she set off travelling.

A sudden cold knot tightened in her stomach, a churning mix of fear and recognition. She'd known this place her whole life, yet stepping into it blind felt like crossing into another world.

'Helpless? No one who knows you would ever think that,' Lila replied, squeezing her hand before getting out of the car.

When Lila guided her out of the passenger seat, the ground felt uneven beneath her shoes, with pebbles shifting and damp earth sinking slightly underfoot. She caught the faintest breath of lavender as her coat brushed the brittle stems by the path—dry now, their summer colour would be long gone but still carrying a whisper of scent. It mingled with the apple in the breeze from the garden.

'Mind the step,' Lila murmured.

Dimity reached forward, fingers brushing the familiar grain of the old wooden door. The paint was peeling—she could feel the flakes catch against her palm.

She stood on the threshold, cane in hand, absorbing the sensations as the cottage door creaked open, unleashing a rush of familiar scents—beeswax polish, old books, the lingering ghost of Aunt Bea's lavender sachets. Before Bea had passed two years ago, Dimity had finished the third novel of her Shadowlands series in that snug study overlooking the back garden. Six months later, she'd left to travel Europe—never imagining it would be her last goodbye to Aunt Bea.

She stepped in, Lila beside her. The floorboards creaked beneath her feet, exactly where she remembered, and she counted her steps by memory—three to the hall table, two more to the edge of the rug. Her fingers found the smooth curve of the banister, worn by generations of hands, and something inside her steadied.

Dimity tapped her cane tentatively, then set it aside. 'I won't need this in here. Three steps to the sitting room. Armchair to the left of the fireplace. Bea's writing desk under the front window. Bookshelf along the right wall.'

She moved forwards confidently, fingers trailing along the wall until she reached the sitting room archway. Seven steps took her to the armchair—a Victorian piece with worn velvet upholstery and curved wooden arms polished smooth by generations of hands. She traced the familiar carved wooden birds that served as finials on each arm—Aunt Bea's "guardian birds", she had called them when she was a child.

'See? I know this place by heart,' Dimity said, turning towards where she knew Lila must be standing. 'It's as familiar to me as my own body. More so, currently, since my body seems to be malfunctioning.'

'Your irreverent humour remains intact, I see,' Lila observed dryly. 'Let's get you properly settled. I told Marcus I'd be here for a couple of days.'

'I knew it would be perfect,' Dimity whispered. 'I can do this. I remember it all, even without being able to see it.'

'You're sure?' Lila asked.

At least I won't get lost in here. The cottage would remember her, even if she couldn't see it. Dimity blinked back tears as she followed Lila from room to room in the tiny cottage.

'You've still got power and hot water,' Lila said. 'It's not been turned off. When I was in the back garden, I spoke to Mrs Willoughby next door—she's been keeping an eye on the place for you. Comes in once a month to air it out and do a bit of dusting. After you called her, she stocked the pantry and left fresh bedding.'

Dimity smiled faintly. The familiar words of her aunt echoed in her head: A good home looks after itself if you love it enough.

'Now, I've put the kettle near the power point next to the sink. It's good that it's one with a base that can be plugged in, so all you'll have to do is lift it up, feel for the tap, fill it up, count to five like we worked out to get it to the right level, and then use your other hand to put it back onto the pad. I've moved all the coffee cups and bowls into the top drawer underneath that part of the kitchen bench. Okay, then— two steps to the left. You've got the fridge, and the milk is at hand height for you. All good?'

'You're an absolute gem, you know that, don't you, Lila? You know I don't count you as my agent so much as one of my closest friends.' She gave a wry chuckle. 'In fact, when I think about it, you're probably the only friend I've got these days.'

Lila reached out, put her hand on Dimity's arm and squeezed gently. 'I'm sure you've got friends at home who care about you. England's a big place, and you've had your head down writing and been busy travelling.'

'The travelling was the best thing for me. Some of those beaches in Croatia inspired my settings. It's a wonder I managed to imagine those settings in my earlier books; the only travel I'd done before I went to Europe was to visit Aunt Bea with Mum every couple of years.'

'I've seen photos of where you live in Australia. Those crater lakes you showed me were stunning. Not to mention all the rainforests.'

Dimity chuckled. 'I spent most of my teenage years in the library at school or in my bedroom reading. I was passionate about becoming a writer, a storyteller.' She stood in the kitchen staring into the darkness she had become used to. 'Poor Mum. All she wanted me to do was work in the local pharmacy when they offered me a job after school. They promised to put me through a course so I could be a dispenser. I couldn't think of anything worse than standing behind a counter all day, talking to people. I just wanted to be in my own head, in my own space, writing stories.'

'Sadly, we all have to have a job and earn money to live,' Lila said.

'Yeah. Mum and Dad were great, though. I did a couple of courses online, and Mum felt as though I was doing something productive then—although she used to talk about my "writing nonsense" and how it was a phase I'd get over.'

'And I guess you've shown her.'

Dimity shook her head slowly. 'Actually, no. I came to England and moved into the cottage briefly after Aunt Bea's funeral, and that's where I finished the third book of Shadowlands before I started travelling and researching locations. When I self-published the first three books, I believed they weren't anywhere near good enough for a publisher to read.'

Lila made a noise between a snort and a grunt. 'And we both know what happened then.'

'Yes, when the sales graph on my e-book sites went up, I had to pinch myself. Then I printed it, and sales on Amazon went through the roof—and suddenly, I had an income, as well as a cottage.

'And what did your mother say about that?'

'Would you believe I haven't told her that I've been successful?'

'What does she think you're doing? How does she think you're supporting yourself?'

'Well, the first couple of weeks I was here, I did get a job waitressing, and I told her about that. She was quite pleased. She sees it as me getting England out of my system before I go home and do something worthwhile.'

'And she thinks you're still waitressing, because you didn't tell her that you weren't?'

Lila's tone was light at first, but Dimity could hear the question beneath it — the gentle disapproval she'd been expecting. She felt Lila's arm shift under her hand, and she tightened her grip without meaning to.

'And I'm assuming you did tell her you were in hospital?'

'Yes. Yesterday. Dr Hughes helped me.'

'Well, that's something, I suppose... and have you told her you're now staying at the cottage?'

'Yes. I told her I was moving back.'

There was a pause—longer this time. When Lila spoke again, her voice had changed; the edge had gone, replaced by quiet worry.

'And you've told her that your vision still hasn't returned?'

Dimity hesitated. The ticking of the clock seemed to grow louder, steady and unrelenting.

The words caught somewhere between her throat and her chest.

There was a long silence.

'I might have implied I was back to normal at the end of the call.'

Lila's hand slid down to hers, squeezing hard.

'Dimity,' she said quietly, 'are you telling me that you're over here and I'm the only one who knows you've lost your vision — that your parents don't know you're living in this cottage completely in the dark?'

'Yes, but I'm fine.'

Lila exhaled sharply, half a sigh, half a laugh. 'Fine? You're on your own in the middle of nowhere, and you think that's fine?'

Dimity stayed quiet, letting Lila's words settle. Concern was easier to hear when it came wrapped in humour.

Lila's tone softened again. 'Dr Hughes might be right — your sight could come back any day. But until then, you'll bunker down here in the cottage you love, eat those microwave meal boxes I left in the freezer—though they might taste like cardboard. I think they're called "easy bites" or something equally tragic.'

Dimity smiled, the sound of Lila's chuckle

easing the tightness in her chest.

'Won't hurt me. Sometimes, when I get into the story, I forget to eat anyway.'

'Well, you won't be doing that, because I'll be ringing you three times every day to check that you've had breakfast, lunch, and dinner — and that you've survived being in the dark.'

'You're a sweetheart, and you know what?'

'What?' Lila said.

'I want you to increase the percentage you're taking from my book sales and the Netflix deal if it goes ahead. Fifteen per cent isn't enough for what you do for me.'

'No way am I doing that. I said this is friendship, not agency. And besides,' — Dimity could hear the grin in her voice — 'Your books are selling like wildfire—you'll be the rich one soon enough. Now that you've given me permission to sign the deal on your behalf, we're on the way, baby. Speaking of which, tomorrow we'll talk about this book and what we're going to do. It will all work out, love. I do not doubt that.'

'It will. I know that too.' Dimity smiled as certainty filled her. The cottage surrounded her once again, just as it always had: not with light, but with love.

Aunty Bea. It was as though she was there.

Chapter Four

By evening, the cottage had begun to breathe around them again. Lila cleaned the kitchen after they had dinner, and then she moved through the cottage, checking cupboards, running the taps. The comforting clatter of domestic noise filled the rooms, driving back the silence that had filled Dimity's mind when she was in the hospital.

The scent of tea drifted across the room—strong, earthy, slightly over-brewed. The scrape of a teaspoon against a cup, the soft clink as Lila set it beside her, added to her comfort.

'Here you go, love. Proper tea. None of that hospital swill.'

Dimity wrapped her hands around the mug, feeling its warmth seep into her palms. 'You make it exactly like Bea did,' she said.

'Then she clearly had excellent taste,' Lila replied dryly.

They sat together for a few minutes, no conversation breaking the silence. Outside, rain began to whisper on the roof, a soft, steady rhythm; Dimity tilted her head, listening. The sound reminded her of long afternoons at Bea's kitchen table, pen scratching across paper, the raindrops keeping time with her thoughts. She sighed, feeling the faint stir of her story beneath her tiredness.

'Something will happen,' Lila murmured, as if reading her mind. 'It always does.'

Dimity smiled. 'You're right.'

'Of course I am,' Lila said, rising. 'Now, bed for you, love. Tomorrow we'll sort your setup—dictation, laptop, whatever it takes.'

When the door clicked softly behind her, Dimity sat for a while longer, her fingers tracing the rim of the cooling cup. The scent of tea and rain filled the room, and in the darkness behind her eyes, a single image flickered to life—her story stirred.

She stood and felt her way to the bedroom she had always slept in on her visits.

The next day passed in a flurry of activity. Lila labelled essentials with tactile markers—raised dots on tinned goods in the pantry, different-shaped labels on bathroom products. They established systems for clothing—separate drawers for each colour, items arranged by type.

In the afternoon, they moved on to practical work: Dimity learned to pour liquids with her finger crooked inside the cup to detect the level, to slice fruit with a hand resting lightly on the board to guide the knife, to count steps from the hallway to the kettle, the cooker, and the back door.

Later, they tested the talking clock and set voice-assistant reminders for medication, meals, and appointments. Lila showed her how to use the new phone Marcus had bought while she was in hospital; the raised case edges helped Dimity find the buttons by touch. By mid-afternoon, she could walk the length of the cottage unaided, up the stairs to her bedroom, each turn and step imprinted on her mind.

When they stopped for tea, the talk turned to the manuscript. The edits were waiting, the deadlines hovering. Lila had been trying to sound practical, but Dimity could hear the worry in her voice — the undercurrent that always surfaced when business collided with friendship.

'You need help,' Lila said finally, the decision landing like a full stop at the end of a long sentence.

'I agree,' Dimity said slowly. 'I do need

someone to help me, and I've had an idea. Someone to take dictation, read back passages, and help me organise my thoughts. Make adjustments to my manuscript.' The idea of another person hearing her unpolished sentences—especially the romantic ones—made her cringe, but necessity had to override artistic pride.

'I could do it—'

'You can't,' Dimity said gently. 'You've got the agency to run, and Marcus needs you at home in London. And besides, you're not an editor.' She reached for Lila's hand, fumbling a little before finding it. 'Just find me someone good. Someone who understands the work and won't flinch when I start talking about magical creatures and sexy scenes. Someone I can trust. Maybe someone who can cook, too.'

'I'll make some calls.'

Dimity listened as Lila crossed to the table, papers rustling, laptop keys clicking. She could hear her brisk confidence as she spoke on the phone; every so often, Lila would pause, murmuring "mm-hmm" or "of course" in that calm, measured voice. Affection for her friend flooded through Dimity.

At last, Lila hung up and turned, her Cockney tones back in place. 'Whitmore & Reed in Oxford—reputable, well-connected. They specialise in supporting authors with all sorts of challenges: disability, translation, and even writers working in their second language. They've suggested someone with exactly the right background.'

'Who?'

'Vivienne Edwards,' Lila said, reading from her notes. 'Available immediately for the six-week period you need. Oxford-educated, several big publishing houses under her belt, experienced in both fantasy world-building and—' she hesitated, then laughed, '—the "romantic" side of things.'

Dimity smiled. 'Another woman will be easier. I'm already dreading dictating some of those raunchy scenes, but at least it won't be quite so mortifying.'

Lila chuckled. 'Apparently, she's used to working with authors who'd rather vanish through the floor than describe a kiss aloud. You'll be in good hands.'

'Go for it,' Dimity said. 'I trust your judgment.'

By the time the arrangements were finalised, the afternoon had moved to evening. They sat before the fire, Lila reading aloud from Dimity's manuscript, discussing plot points and character arcs.

'You were right,' Lila admitted, setting the pages aside. 'This is some of your best work. The battle scene in the Thornwood Forest is absolutely gripping, and the tension between Elara and Lord Ashton—well, it's impossible to put down.'

'I imagined it all here and wrote it as I travelled.' Dimity curled deeper into Aunt Bea's armchair. 'It's always been magical, this cottage. Bea swore it had special properties.' She laughed softly. 'She claimed it could see into people's hearts, know what they needed before they did themselves. My fingers are itching to get to work.'

'That's fabulous. And it sounds like your great-aunt was a romantic,' Lila said fondly.

'She found love here,' Dimity pointed out. 'Middle-aged, convinced she'd be forever alone, then suddenly—Arthur appears in the village, his car broken down outside her gate.'

'Coincidence.'

'Bea never thought so. She always said the cottage brought them together. Said it had Christmas magic, especially—that it helps those who live here, guides them towards what they need.'

'Like a benevolent spirit?'

'Or a ghost, or a ley line, or simply very old stones that have absorbed centuries of love and intention.' Dimity shrugged. 'Bea never tried to explain it. She just believed.'

There was a smile in Lila's voice. 'If it is a ley line, it's a gentle one. No strange lights or humming stones—just calm.'

Dimity tilted her head, listening to the faint sigh of wind against the windowpanes. 'Bea used to say you could feel it if you were still enough— the way the air seems to hold its breath, as though the house is listening.'

'And do you?'

She hesitated. The warmth from the fire brushed her face, mingling with the faint scent of lavender and old wood polish. 'Maybe. It feels… familiar. As if the house remembers.'

Lila reached across and squeezed her hand.

Dimity smiled faintly. 'Bea always said places carry what we leave behind—the good moments, the love, the laughter. Maybe that's the only kind of magic there is.'

Lila didn't answer, but Dimity heard her exhale softly. For a while, only the hiss of the fire filled the room. She leaned back, letting her fingers trace the curve of the armrest again. Every hollow and dent in the timber felt like a story waiting to be uncovered. The thought steadied her. The cottage had seen other beginnings, other returns. Perhaps it remembered those, too—the quiet rhythm of love, the persistence of words finding their way onto the page.

Later, in the kitchen, they drank cocoa from heavy mugs while Lila reviewed her list one final time.

'The agency will invoice you monthly,' Lila said. 'Mrs Willoughby has agreed to shop twice a week, and I've arranged a car service for your first appointment with Dr Hughes. I'm sorry we'll be away that week, but you ring me as soon as you see him. Your new phone's voice-activated. And I'm just a call away if—'

'I'll be fine,' Dimity interrupted gently. 'Everything's arranged. Vivienne arrives tomorrow, and the cottage knows me. It'll look after me.'

Lila sighed. 'You're starting to sound like your aunt.'

'Worse things to sound like.' Dimity reached across the table, finding Lila's hand after only a slight fumble. 'Thank you. For everything.'

'Just finish that manuscript,' Lila said, squeezing her fingers. 'I need to know if Elara chooses the knight or the fae lord.'

'You'll have to wait like everyone else,' Dimity teased.

They laughed together. Then Lila got up from her chair—footsteps crossing to the window, the faint creak of floorboards marking her path.

'It's snowing,' she said softly.

Dimity could sense it too, not by sight but by the hush that settled over the cottage, the softened crackle of the fire, the muffled quiet beyond the walls.

'I know,' Dimity whispered. She tilted her face towards the soundless world, the air pressing close and calm. 'I can feel it.'

The fire popped once, and the cottage seemed to sigh, as though content that its walls were full again—of warmth and voices. Maybe even hope.

Chapter Five

By midmorning the next day, the cottage smelled faintly of toast and polish. Lila moved through the rooms methodically, checking lists and testing light switches one last time.

'You've got the emergency numbers in your phone. Just "hey Siri", if you need them,' she said. 'And Mrs Willoughby's number is there too. She said she'll pop over most days, but make sure you call me if anything feels off?'

'I promise,' Dimity said. She stood by the doorway, one hand resting on the frame, the other holding her cane. 'You've thought of everything, Lila. I'll be fine.'

Lila hesitated. 'It's only that... it's early days. You tire easily, and—well, this is a big step.'

'I know.' Dimity smiled at the sound of her friend fussing with her bag. 'But I need to start living here, not just existing. I'll manage.'

Lila's sigh softened into a laugh. 'You always do. And you keep me up to date with the flashes and anything else with your vision. Promise?' She squeezed Dimity's arm, the floral scent of her perfume lingering as she opened the front door.

'Of course I will.'

'And the main thing, I want a report on Vivienne as soon as she arrives. Promise? If she doesn't feel right, we'll get someone else.'

'You worry too much.' Dimity smiled as Lila hugged her.

'We'll see you soon. We'll be down in a couple of weeks. And—'

'And I've got six weeks to get this book to you.'

'You take care of yourself, love. You amaze me.'

Dimity blinked back tears as Lila stepped away. She stayed at the door, pausing on the threshold. The air outside was cold against her cheeks, carrying the faint scent of frost and woodsmoke. Gravel shifted beneath Lila's feet, then the muffled thud of the car door closing. The engine started, low and steady, followed by the crunch of tyres as it rolled down the lane, followed by a happy toot of the horn as Lila turned onto the road.

She stood listening until the sound faded completely, leaving only the stillness of the morning—the drip of melting frost from the eaves, the distant caw of a rook in the trees beyond the garden. The silence pressed close, suddenly unfamiliar.

For a brief moment, unease flickered. The cottage was too quiet, as if holding its breath. Then the warmth from the hearth reached her where she stood, and the familiar scent of beeswax and old books drifted out to meet her.

Dimity exhaled slowly, grounding herself in the small, familiar sounds: the tick of the kitchen clock, the soft creak of timber beneath her feet, the whisper of wind against the windowpanes. She wasn't alone—the cottage was here waiting, just as it always had been.

'All right, Bea,' she murmured. 'It's just me now.'

She closed the door gently, feeling for the latch until it clicked home, and stood a moment longer, palms pressed to the wood, steadying herself against the quiet that no longer felt like loneliness but like belonging.

A knock came at the back door not long after she made her way to the kitchen. Mrs

Willoughby's cheerful voice floated in before Dimity reached it.

'Just checking you're all right, dear. I heard your friend's car go down the lane. Thought you might like a bit of company.'

Dimity ushered her in, feeling steadier already. The older woman's clothes rustled as she shrugged off her coat, bringing with her the scent of outside—cold air and woodsmoke. 'Sit down, Mrs Willoughby. Let me make us some tea.'

She found the kettle by touch, the familiar smoothness of its handle beneath her palm, then reached for the tin of tea leaves marked with a raised dot. Water poured cleanly into the pot, her finger resting lightly against the rim to gauge the level. The sound of it gave her confidence.

'Fruit cake?' she asked. 'I think I know where Lila left it.'

Mrs Willoughby chuckled. 'You sound as though you've been here a month already.'

By the time Dimity set the tray on the table, the tremor in her hands had eased. Each small task—slicing the cake, positioning the plates, pouring without spilling—was a small victory.

They talked about the village, the weather,

and the quiet lane that led to the churchyard. How much Mrs Willoughby missed Bea. And how much Bea had missed Arthur when he'd passed. Dimity listened to the rise and fall of her neighbour's voice, taking comfort in its steadiness, and knowing that her cottage was only a few steps away.

When the older woman left, the house felt comfortable rather than empty.

She had just put the cups into the sink when the phone buzzed in her pocket. The voice assistant read out her mother's name, and a familiar tightness coiled in her chest. As she answered, she made her way to the chair in the sitting room and eased herself down. A reassuring double flash of light pierced the darkness as she leaned back.

'Hi, Mum.'

'Dimity! Finally. How are you, darling? You sound better. Have you recovered properly now?'

'I'm fine,' she said lightly. 'Still a bit tired, but much better.'

'That's good to hear. You'll be coming home soon, won't you? Once you've got your strength back?'

Dimity hesitated. If I tell her the truth, she thought, she'll panic. She'll be on the next flight. She'll insist on taking over, fussing, and deciding everything for me. I can't bear that—not yet. Not when I'm still figuring out who I am in the dark.

'I think it's better if I stay put for a while,' she said carefully.

Her mother's voice sharpened. 'Stay put? Where exactly are you?'

'At Aunt Bea's cottage. I mean my cottage. Pippin's Nook.'

A beat of silence. Then, clipped and incredulous: 'You're back there?'

'Yes. It's peaceful, and I have a novel to write. It feels right to be here.'

'Write?' Her mother gave a short, disbelieving laugh. 'You should be resting, not working. You've been in hospital, Dimity. You need proper care, not to bury yourself in that draughty old place.'

'I'm fine, Mum. Really.'

'That's not the point,' her mother snapped, and then, more tightly controlled: 'I don't understand why you insist on making things difficult. You could come home, recover properly, and see your family and friends again.

Why hide away over there?'

Dimity pressed her hand against the carved edge of the armrest, grounding herself. Because if you knew I'd lost my sight, you'd never let me stay. Because I need to recover before I can face you.

'It's not hiding,' she said evenly. 'It's living. I love it here.'

Her mother made a small sound—half sigh, half frustration. 'When will you stop being so independent? You can't just decide to stay there forever.'

'I haven't decided anything.'

'Well, it's nearly Christmas. You'll come home by then, surely? Your sisters are keen to see you. Did I tell you Christie is pregnant again?'

'I don't think so.'

'The silence that followed was the kind Dimity had known all her life—heavy, full of things neither of them ever managed to say.

'Mum, I'm twenty-four,' Dimity said quietly. 'I might not come home again—not to live there, anyway.'

Her mother's breath caught. 'Don't be ridiculous. You're still not yourself. We'll talk about this when you're thinking clearly.'

'I am thinking clearly,' Dimity said softly. 'For the first time in a long while.'

For a moment, she thought she heard her mother's breath catch, a tiny sound that almost broke her resolve. Then the familiar distance returned, crisp and polite.

'Well,' her mother said at last. 'If that's how you feel.'

'It is. But I'll call again soon.'

When the call ended, she stood for a long moment in the stillness, the faint hum of the fridge and the soft tick of the clock filling the quiet her mother had left behind.

She'll never understand, Dimity thought. Not until she has to.

After the call, she wandered the cottage alone, trailing her fingers along walls and furniture, reconfirming her mental map. In the study, she touched the laptop she could no longer use, the notebooks filled with her handwriting and sketches of fantastical creatures, now inaccessible to her. The tactile markers on the telephone, the voice-activated digital assistant set up beside her favourite reading chair.

'Well, Bea,' she said aloud to the empty

cottage, 'it's just us now. And soon, Vivienne. Let's hope she's patient. The cottage will tell me, won't it?' The wind sighed outside as if in affirmation, and Dimity smiled.

She made herself tea, counting spoons of leaves into the pot. Small victories. Independence preserved in tiny increments.

In the sitting room, she curled into the armchair, fingers absently tracing the wooden birds on the armrests, reminiscing. The scent of beeswax polish and old books comforted her, grounding her in memories of childhood visits— Aunt Bea reading stories by the fire, teaching her to bake in the cottage's Aga stove, showing her how to identify flowers in the garden by scent and texture alone.

'I wish you were here,' Dimity whispered. 'You'd know how to make this right.'

A sudden waft of vanilla and almond—the unmistakable scent of Aunt Bea's Christmas biscuits—drifted through the room. Dimity sat up straighter, puzzled. The kitchen was empty, the Aga cold. The biscuits were a Christmas tradition she and Bea had always made together, the recipe a family secret.

The cottage helping, she thought, then

immediately dismissed it as wishful thinking.

Before she could ponder the phantom scent further, a knock sounded at the cottage door.

Chapter Six

Three sharp raps, then two gentle ones.

Dimity rose, smoothing her cashmere jumper nervously, and made her way carefully to the door. Seven steps from armchair to archway, fourteen more across the entryway. She'd opted not to use her cane inside the cottage, determined to navigate her familiar space independently.

Drawing a steadying breath, she unlatched the door and pulled it open, feeling a rush of cold air carrying the scent of snow and pine.

'Ms Armstrong? I'm Vivian Edwards from Whitmore & Reed. Sorry if I'm a few minutes late—the snow's making the lanes rather treacherous.'

Dimity frowned. The voice was smooth and cultured—but much deeper than she'd expected. A ripple of confusion passed through her, followed by a sharp, physical stillness. Then the realisation hit.

Her rehearsed greeting died on her lips. The voice that addressed her was unmistakably, unquestionably male—a rich baritone with traces of a Northern accent softening the precise Oxford diction.

'I—there must be some mistake,' she managed, her hand tightening on the doorframe. 'I was expecting . . . a . . . Vivienne Edwards.'

A pause. Then a warm chuckle. 'Ah, the eternal confusion. It's Vivian—V-i-v-i-a-n. Rather like Evelyn or Hilary—one of those names that swung from predominantly male to female, or in my case, hasn't quite decided. My parents were traditionalists who preferred the original masculine spelling.'

Dimity's pulse kicked hard against her ribs. A man. They'd sent a man. For a moment, she thought absurdly of the half-written scenes in her manuscript, of Elara and Lord Ashton, of hands and breath, kisses and much more. Explicit words she'd never intended to speak aloud to anyone.

'There's been a misunderstanding.'

'That I'm male?' Vivian replied, tone still pleasant but edged with professional distance. 'I assure you I'm experienced with a wide range of content, including fantasy world-building and romantic themes. But if you prefer a female editor, I understand. The agency can send someone else, though it may take several days to arrange.'

Several days. The thought struck like a closing door—the deadline, the empty house, the unfinished story waiting upstairs. She didn't have several days to play with.

Dimity straightened her shoulders. 'No, that won't be necessary. Please, come in, Mr Edwards. The weather sounds dreadful.'

'Vivian, please,' he said, stamping snow from his boots before stepping inside. 'It's rather coming down out there—winter's not far off.'

The scent of cold air, wool, and something clean and citrusy came in with him, unsettling in its unfamiliar warmth.

Dimity closed the door, turning towards his voice. 'I apologise for the confusion,' she said, extending her hand in his direction. 'Dimity Armstrong. Welcome to Pippin's Nook.'

His hand engulfed hers—large, warm, callused. Not what she'd expected from an editor. 'Pleasure to meet you properly. I've admired your work for some time.'

'You've read my books?' Dimity couldn't hide the surprise.

'All four in the Chronicles of the Shadowlands series,' Vivian confirmed. 'Brilliant balance of epic fantasy and romance. Your world-building is extraordinary—the way you've layered the political intrigue of the different courts whilst maintaining that sense of wonder in the magic. It's Narnia meets *A Song of Ice and Fire*, but entirely your own.'

The compliment hit with surprising force, and heat rose to her cheeks as he followed her in. 'Well,' she murmured, 'thank you. That's precisely what I was trying to do.'

An awkward silence followed. The cottage seemed smaller with him there—his voice came from well above her own height, and the room seemed to be filled with energy.

'Perhaps I could take your coat?' she offered, clinging to formality. 'And show you around— well, not show exactly, but—'

'Guide me through?' Vivian suggested kindly. 'That would be helpful.'

The rustle of heavy fabric as he removed his coat, the subtle shifting of air as he moved. Dimity held out her hand, and after a brief hesitation, he placed the coat in it—heavier than expected, wool with what felt like a waterproof outer layer. She hung it on the coat rack beside the door, proud when she found the hook on the first try.

'The cottage is small but easy to get around,' she began, turning back towards him. 'Sitting room through here, kitchen beyond that. Study to the right, stairs to the left leading to two bedrooms and a bath. I've prepared the blue bedroom for you, assuming you'll stay on-site as we discussed with the agency. The village has limited accommodation otherwise, especially in winter.'

'As long as you are comfortable with me staying? I can give you some referees to call, if that makes you feel more at ease?'

'You came highly recommended, Mr Edwards. That is enough.'

'On-site would be ideal for the work schedule that was outlined,' Vivian agreed, following her into the sitting room. 'I believe there is a tight deadline.'

'That's correct. We'll start work early tomorrow.' Dimity moved with confidence through the cottage, describing each room and its function, her fingers trailing along surfaces for reassurance. She explained the systems Lila had established—the tactile markers, the organisation of household essentials, the voice-activated technology.

In the study, Dimity paused, her fingers finding the familiar grain of Bea's writing desk. She traced the brass handles of the drawers, remembering afternoons spent here as a child, watching her aunt sort through papers and correspondence. Somewhere in the bottom drawer were Arthur's letters—the ones he'd written during the war, tied with faded ribbon. Bea had shown them to her once, years ago, but Dimity had never read them. They'd felt too private —a love story that belonged to Bea and Arthur alone. Perhaps one day, when she was ready, she'd read them.

She moved to the desk where her laptop sat. 'This is where we'll work. I have about three-quarters of the manuscript completed, but it's on my computer, which is... well, rather useless to me now.'

'I've brought equipment to help with that,' Vivian said, moving to stand beside her—not too close, she noted, respecting her space. 'Software that can extract your existing text, dictation programs, and specialised editing tools. The agency mentioned you prefer to work mornings?'

'Yes. My brain functions best before lunch,' Dimity confirmed. 'Though I'm flexible, given the deadline constraints. We should probably have a break and work in the afternoons too.'

'We'll establish a routine that works for both of us,' he assured her. 'Starting tomorrow, if that suits? Today, perhaps you could familiarise me with your manuscript's current state, your plans for the remaining chapters?'

The prospect of diving immediately into her work—the romantic scenes, the complex magical systems—with this stranger whose face she couldn't even see made Dimity's stomach tighten with anxiety. But professionalism demanded she push through her discomfort.

'Of course,' she said, more firmly than she felt. 'Though I should warn you, this instalment involves Elara finally confronting her feelings for both potential suitors. There are some rather... intimate scenes.'

'I assure you, Ms Armstrong—'

'Dimity, please.'

'Dimity. I assure you I'm entirely professional about content of any nature. Your words are just that—words. Necessary components of your artistic expression and your characters' development.'

His voice held no embarrassment and no judgment, and that somehow eased her tension slightly. Whatever his appearance—and Dimity found herself intensely curious about the physical person attached to that rich voice—Vivian Edwards was clearly a professional.

'Right,' she nodded decisively. 'Tea first, I think, then we'll discuss plot structure. The kettle's just boiled before you arrived.'

As she moved towards the kitchen, warmth seemed to emanate from the cottage walls—the old heating system kicking in, perhaps, though it had never been particularly efficient. The scent of almond and vanilla briefly returned, then faded.

In the kitchen doorway, Dimity paused, a strange certainty washing over her that this unexpected development—a male editor instead of female—was somehow what was meant to happen. Almost as if the cottage itself had arranged it. Why on earth would she think that?

The cottage helping those who live here, Bea's voice whispered in her memory.

'Ridiculous,' she murmured to herself.

'I'm sorry?' Vivian asked from behind her.

'Nothing,' Dimity replied quickly. 'Just talking to the cottage. Old habit from childhood visits. Aunt Bea always said it was listening.'

To her surprise, Vivian didn't laugh. 'The best old houses do have personalities of their own, I've found. I look forward to getting acquainted with this one.'

Perhaps this unexpected arrangement would work after all.

Nothing to do with the warm baritone voice, the large, gentle hands, or the subtle scent of citrus and wool that now mingled with the cottage's familiar aromas. She was beginning to like him already.

As evening settled over the cottage, Dimity showed Vivian upstairs to the blue bedroom. 'It's the larger of the two guest rooms,' she explained, trailing her fingers along the banister. 'The bathroom is just across the hall. I've left towels on the bed.'

'It's perfect,' Vivian assured her. 'Thank you.'

They shared a simple supper—soup that Mrs Willoughby had left, bread from the village bakery. The conversation stayed light and professional as they settled into the reality of working side by side.

'I do have one more question,' she asked as he stood to clear the table.

'Can you cook?'

The laughter in his voice was clear. 'Very well,' he said.

When Dimity finally retreated to her own room, she could hear Vivian moving about upstairs, the old floorboards creaking under his weight.

She smiled when she remembered she was supposed to call Lila. It was too late to call, so she dictated a text into her phone and asked Siri to send it to Lila.

MISTER ViviAN Edwards will do nicely. And he can cook too. No need to check up on me. I'll call you.

Chapter Seven

Morning crept quietly into Pippin's Nook. The old place had its quirks—doors that stuck in damp weather and floorboards that creaked in different places every day as the mood took them. The wind rattled the window frames, and the fire in the sitting room below popped loudly, the warmth pervading the cottage. From the kitchen came the steady whistle of the kettle and, faintly, a voice.

Dimity blinked, momentarily disoriented. For a few seconds, she couldn't remember where she was, then the familiar scents of polish, tea, and woodsmoke settled her. Downstairs, it was Vivian reading.

She dressed quickly, hoping that she had chosen matching colours, and then followed the familiar path to the stairs, one hand brushing the banister. Her slippered feet found each step without hesitation, the rhythmic creak of wood guiding her.

In the kitchen, the smell of freshly-steeped tea met her. 'Good morning, Dimity,' Vivian said easily, as though breakfast together was a regular occurrence. 'I've made us some breakfast—toast and marmalade. I hope that suits you.'

'It's perfect,' she replied, responding to the ease in his tone, thinking it would be easy to eat without having food stick to her face.

They ate quietly, the fire crackling back to life behind them. The comfort felt strange — a man she'd met only yesterday moving through her kitchen with the familiarity of someone who belonged there.

When they began work, Vivian suggested starting by reading through her existing manuscript. Dimity sat in Aunt Bea's armchair with her notebook open, pen poised more out of habit than necessity.

His voice filled the room, unexpectedly resonant. Words she had written months ago took on new life through his cadence: her dialogue sounded truer, her characters painted more vividly. It was disconcerting and oddly intimate to hear her own imagination filtered through another person's voice.

Then he reached one of the more . . . um . . . hotter passages. The touching, the breathing, the kiss . . . the rest.

Warmth crept up her neck as Vivian read from the screen—Elara's whispered surrender, Lord Ashton's name caught between her moans. His delivery stayed measured, almost businesslike, yet the low register of his voice sent an involuntary shiver down Dimity's spine. Did that make him confident, she wondered, or was he simply untouched by the intimacy of the scene?

'Shall I continue?' Vivian asked when the silence stretched a little too long.

'Yes, please,' she said quickly.

By mid-morning, they had settled into an easy rhythm. She dictated new paragraphs, haltingly at first, gaining confidence as Vivian typed. His occasional questions — thoughtful and focused—revealed an editor's mind attuned to emotion as well as correct grammar.

The gentle knock at the back door startled them both.

Mrs Willoughby bustled in without waiting for an answer, her arms full of groceries and her voice full of cheer. 'Morning, dear! I brought you some bread from the bakery and a few things for your pantry.'

'Mrs Willoughby, you're an angel,' Dimity said, rising to greet her.

The older woman's attention quickly shifted to Vivian. 'And you must be the helper Lila mentioned. Well, don't you bring a bit of sunshine into this place!'

Vivian laughed softly. 'I do my best, ma'am.'

'Call me Iris, everyone does,' she said briskly. 'Lovely to see Pippin's Nook lively again. You know, Beatrice always said this place had a way of bringing the right people together at just the right time.'

'Perhaps it simply rewards kindness,' Vivian said mildly, but Dimity heard the smile in his voice.

Iris chuckled. 'You keep telling yourself that, young man.'

When she turned to go, Dimity insisted on seeing her out. But as she reached for the kitchen door, it refused to budge. She frowned, pulling harder. 'It's stuck.'

'Let me,' Vivian said, stepping close. He reached past her, his arm brushing hers, his shirt sleeve grazing the back of her hand. The scent of his cologne filled the small space. Together they pushed, the wood groaning before finally giving way.

For a moment, neither spoke. The air between them felt charged, alive. Then Vivian stepped back, clearing his throat. 'Old timber,' he said lightly. 'Always shifts with the weather.'

'Of course,' Dimity murmured, though she wasn't convinced the cottage hadn't chosen that exact moment to intervene.

After Mrs Willoughby's departure, they returned to the study. The work resumed—Dimity dictating, his quiet typing punctuated by the occasional suggestion. The fire burned steadily, and behind her eyelids, pinpricks of light flashed, turning gold.

She frowned slightly, tilting her head towards the window. Where was the gold coming from?

'May I describe the sunset to you?' Vivian asked softly.

She turned towards his voice, pulse quickening. 'Please.'

He was quiet for a moment, and she could hear the shift in his breathing—slower, deeper, as though he were gathering the scene into himself before offering it to her.

'The sky is on fire,' he began, his voice low and unhurried. 'Not the angry kind—the sort that warms you from the inside. The whole horizon's burning gold, spilling through the bare branches of the orchard like molten light through lace. The snow's caught it—every drift, every ridge—so the garden looks as though it's been dipped in golden honey.'

Dimity's breath caught. The gold behind her eyes pulsed, brighter now, as if responding to his words.

He continued, his tone softening. 'There's amber at the edges, fading into rose where the clouds have gathered. And above it all, the sky's turning violet—deep and cool, like the colour that lives just beneath the surface of the air. It's the kind of light that makes you believe in something you can't name.'

She sat perfectly still, afraid to move, afraid to break whatever was happening. The gold intensified, spreading, and for the briefest moment, she saw shapes moving—soft, radiant, alive.

'That was beautiful,' she whispered. 'You should be a writer, Vivian. Truly.'

The silence that followed was charged.

His chair creaked as he shifted, and when he spoke, his voice had changed—flat where it had been warm, careful where it had been free.

'The light's fading now,' he said. 'We should get back to work.'

'Vivian?' She turned towards him, concern cutting through her wonder. 'What's wrong?'

'Nothing's wrong,' he said briskly. 'Just . . . we've lost the daylight. Best to continue while we can still see the page.'

But she heard what he didn't say. Something in her words had bothered him, and the golden world he'd painted for her had taken something with it when it disappeared.

Just as Dimity reached for her tea, a faint creak echoed through the room. She turned towards the sound—the study door, moving on its own, just enough to let in a soft draught. A single page of her manuscript fluttered free, landing at her feet.

Vivian stooped to retrieve it, and his hand brushed hers. 'Persistent little thing,' he said, setting it neatly back on the pile.

But Dimity only smiled to herself. The cottage, she thought, was already at work.

***

By evening, the fire had burned low again, throwing soft gold across the sitting room walls.

The day's rhythm had soothed her — the cadence of Vivian's voice reading, the gentle tap of his keyboard, the faint rustle as he turned pages. It had been, she realised, one of the most productive days she'd ever had. Inspiration had filled her, and Dimity knew she could thank Vivian and his melodious voice for that.

Now the cottage was quiet. After they had eaten the meal that Mrs Willoughby had kindly dropped in, Vivian had retreated to the guest room with his laptop and notes, and she had lingered by the fire, unwilling to break the spell the day had woven. Hope filled her as shapes and colours whirled behind her closed eyelids.

Please, oh, please.

She leaned back in Aunt Bea's armchair, fingers resting on the carved wooden birds at each end. The wood was warm from her touch, smooth from years of use. The cottage hummed softly, sounds of memories.

She could almost hear the house breathing — the gentle pop of settling timbers, the sigh of wind through the eaves, the faint pulse of warmth from the embers. Beneath it all lay the memory of Vivian's voice, deep and even, carrying her words into the air as if they were his own thoughts.

It had unsettled her at first, that voice—such self-assurance. Yet the more Vivian spoke, the less her self-consciousness had gripped her. His presence had filled the room without overwhelming her. They had worked well together, anticipating each other's words as they were spoken.

When he read her romantic scenes aloud, something in her had tightened; a strange flutter she couldn't quite name. His voice conveyed the exact feelings she had been trying to write.

She rubbed her thumb over the carved wing of one bird and smiled faintly. Bea would have had something to say about that. The house knows what we need before we do, her aunt had always insisted.

Dimity lifted her face, catching the faint scent of vanilla and almond drifting through the air. It was gone as quickly as it came, leaving her wondering if she'd imagined it.

Upstairs, she could hear faint movement: Vivian closing a drawer, the muffled sound of his footsteps as he crossed the landing. It was comforting, knowing she wasn't alone.

She rose and made her way to the bottom of

the stairs. 'Goodnight, Vivian,' she called softly.

His voice floated down, warm and courteous. 'Goodnight, Dimity. Sleep well.'

The sound lingered after he'd gone still, as though the cottage itself had absorbed it. She climbed the stairs slowly, one hand trailing the banister.

In her bedroom, she undressed by touch and found her way beneath the quilt. The sheets smelled of lavender and starch. The wind moved gently outside, the bare boughs brushing the windows. It was a comforting sound.

Her phone pinged as she drifted off, and she asked Siri to play the voice message.

Note received. Do try to keep your hands on the keyboard and off the editor. I need that manuscript, not wedding invitations. Lila x

Chapter Eight

The next morning, frost rimmed the edges of the windows, and a thin mist drifted across the orchard beyond the garden wall. Somewhere outside, a robin trilled brightly, defying the chill.

How did I know that, Dimity asked herself as she came awake. It was as though the cottage told her what the day was like.

The familiar smell of coffee and toast, and the faint clatter of crockery, drifted up from downstairs. The domestic sounds drew a smile to her face. It had been a long time since she'd woken to another person's movements; one romantic relationship in her early twenties hadn't lasted long, but it had given her enough experience for writing realistic love scenes.

By the time she reached the kitchen, Vivian had brewed coffee. 'Good morning,' he said, voice gentle, unhurried. 'I hope I didn't wake you. I thought coffee this morning would keep us going a little longer.'

'You could wake the dead with that beautiful aroma,' she said, amused. 'Coffee is perfect.

Thank you, you are a mind reader.'

They'd barely settled at the table when Dimity's phone chimed with Lila's distinctive ringtone.

'Sorry, do you mind?' Dimity said in Vivian's direction. 'It's Lila.'

'Of course. Take your time,' he said, and she heard him rise and move away, giving her space.

'Lila, good morning.'

'Dimity! How's it all going? Is everything working out? Can you find everything I set up for you?'

'Everything's perfect,' Dimity said warmly. 'All your tactile markers are exactly where I need them. I'm coping brilliantly.'

'And the editor? Is he being professional? Respectful?'

'Lila, nothing but kind. Actually, that's why I'm calling—well, why you're calling. Like I said in my text, there's no need to ring three times a day to check on me.'

'But we agreed—'

'I know what we agreed, but there's no need. Vivian is looking after me very well. He can cook, too, he said. Mrs Willoughby has been looking after us too.'

'Cook? The perfect man. I must tell Marcus. Speaking of your editor,' Lila continued, her voice taking on a mischievous note. 'I was curious, so I looked him up. Found a photo from an awards ceremony—he won Editor of the Year last year, did you know?'

'No, but yes, very good,' Dimity said carefully.

'Dimity. Girl, he is drop-dead gorgeous.'

Dimity pulled at the polo neck. Her face was flaming hot now. 'Okay, so tell me.'

'Tall—you probably know that already. Dark hair, a bit of a wave to it. Strong jaw. And these eyes—sort of grey-green, very intense. He looks like he walked straight out of one of your novels. Seriously, if Lord Ashton were real and worked in publishing—'

'Lila—'

'I'm just saying! You're alone in a cottage with a man who looks like that and has a voice like melted chocolate? How's the editing going, by the way? Have you reached any of the spicier scenes yet?'

Dimity closed her eyes. 'Yes, excellent progress.'

'That's not an answer. Has he read the library

scene? You know, where Elara and Lord Ashton—'

'The editing is going very well,' Dimity said firmly, though she couldn't suppress her smile. 'Vivian is very good at what he does.'

'I'm sure he is,' Lila said, her grin audible. 'Very good, you say?'

'At editing, Lila.'

'Mmm-hmm. Well, just so you know, I'm only a phone call away if you need anything. Or if anything interesting develops. I'm very invested now.'

'Goodbye, Lila.'

'Have fun with those explicit scenes, darling!'

Dimity ended the call, shaking her head, unable to stop chuckling.

'Everything all right?' Vivian's voice came from nearby. He must have returned to the table.

'Lila wanted to make sure I was managing without her,' Dimity said, her cheeks still warm.

'And are you?'

'Very well, thank you.'

There was a pause, then his voice came quieter, warmer: 'You should smile like that more often. It suits you.'

The warmth in Dimity's cheeks intensified. 'Shall we start? I believe we left off just before Chapter Twelve.'

The morning passed quickly as they worked in the study. Vivian read passages she'd dictated the day before, his voice steady, occasionally pausing to ask questions or offer subtle corrections.

After a while, he set his pen down. 'May I ask you something?'

'Of course.'

He hesitated as though he didn't want to overstep a mark. 'This cottage… it's remarkable. The atmosphere, the stillness. Was it always like this? You mentioned your aunt believed it was special.'

Dimity smiled faintly. 'Bea always said the village was enchanted and each cottage had a soul. She and my great-uncle Arthur met because of it, according to the story. His car broke down right outside that gate —' she gestured instinctively '— and she invited him in for tea. He never really left.'

Vivian's tone softened. 'That sounds like a romance out of one of your books.'

'She thought so too. Said the house had

chosen him.'

'She believed that?'

'She did. She believed the village has its own sort of magic—not the kind with spells or ghosts, but the kind that nudges people where they're meant to go.' Dimity ran her fingers along the edge of the desk. 'There are more stories about it. Couples who visited here for a holiday and ended up engaged. People who arrived broken-hearted and left somehow whole again.'

Vivian gave a quiet laugh, but it wasn't unkind. 'And do you believe that?'

'I didn't,' she admitted. 'Not really. But since coming back...' She hesitated, aware of the warmth that seemed to settle around them. 'Sometimes I sense the house listening. Do I sound crazy?'

A faint creak answered from somewhere behind them, and she smiled. 'See? I rest my case.'

He chuckled, a low, pleasant sound. 'Coincidence.'

'That's what I told Bea,' she said lightly. 'She never agreed, and I think now I have accepted her way of thinking, even if it is a fantasy, it's a happy one.'

She heard the faint scuff of Vivian's chair as he moved. 'Are there pens in one of the desk drawers? Strangely, mine seems to have run out of ink. It's a new one, too.'

'Of course.'

She listened as he crossed the room, his steps deliberate, the sound of drawers sliding open, paper rustling. Then he stopped.

'Dimity,' Vivian said quietly, 'There's something in the back of this drawer. Letters tied with ribbon, and some photographs.'

Her breath caught. 'That would be Arthur's letters.'

'You knew they were here?'

'Yes. Bea showed them to me years ago, but I've never...' She hesitated. 'I've never been able to bring myself to read them. They were too precious to her. It felt like intruding.' Her pulse quickened. 'Describe the photos. I haven't ever seen them.'

He hesitated, then spoke softly. 'A photograph of a woman—she must be your great aunt, judging by the resemblance. She's standing in the garden, holding a basket of apples. There's a man beside her, tall, smiling. And these—' paper rustled '—old letters, tied with a ribbon.'

Dimity reached out instinctively, her hand brushing the edge of the drawer. The paper beneath her fingertips was brittle, the ribbon soft from age.

'Arthur wrote to her after the war,' she murmured, remembering the stories Bea had told. 'They were apart for nearly two years before he came back to her. She said she kept every letter because they were proof that love could survive distance and doubt.'

Vivian didn't speak. The only sound was the faint crackle of the fire. Then, quietly, 'Would you like me to read one to you?'

She nodded. 'I would, if you don't mind.'

He untied the ribbon, and the paper rustled softly as he unfolded the first sheet and then read the words written long ago.

'My dearest Bea,
The frost has settled thick this morning, and I find myself thinking of you in that golden house with the apple trees. Every man here carries something to keep him warm — a photograph, a ribbon, a memory. You are all three to me.'
Vivian's voice faltered slightly at that line, and Dimity's breath caught. She could almost see it—Bea sitting right where she was now,

reading those same words many years ago, the same fire flickering in the grate. She heard the whisper of paper as Vivian carefully refolded the letter, his movements slow, reverent.

When he finished, silence settled again, deeper this time.

'That's beautiful,' Vivian said softly. 'They must have loved each other very much.'

'They did,' Dimity whispered. 'And somehow, I think they still do. In a way.'

She turned her face towards the window. For a fleeting moment, she saw a shape—a wash of rose gold, the faint shimmer of green. It vanished almost immediately, leaving only darkness and the echo of her own breath.

Her heart stuttered. Another shape—but real. More than the pinpricks of light she'd experienced before. This time, there was colour, actual colour. Her hands gripped the armrests of the chair.

My sight is coming back, she thought, hardly daring to believe it. Dr Hughes had said to watch for these moments, that they could signal the brain healing, the return of her sight. Should she call him? Tell Lila? Tell Vivian?

But she said nothing. Not yet. It might have

been wishful thinking, her desperate mind conjuring what it most wanted to see. Better to wait, to see if it happened again, before raising anyone's hopes—especially her own.

'It's extraordinary,' he said. 'You can feel the history here. As if the cottage has experienced a lot of love.'

Dimity smiled faintly. 'It has.'

Outside, the robin sang again, filling Dimity with hope. She'd come home to the right place. And Vivian—this tall, deep-voiced man who made her steamy prose sound even more dangerous—wasn't at all the problem she'd anticipated. She caught herself thinking of Lila's description of him: dark hair, grey-green eyes...

Maybe one day soon, she would see for herself.

Chapter Nine

It was late afternoon by the time they stopped working. Vivian stood and stretched, and the fragrance of his cologne drifted over to Dimity before she heard his footsteps cross to the window.

'It's a silvery dusk tonight and the mist that's hovered over the orchard all afternoon is now pressing close to the window, blurring the world into shades of pearl and shadow.' She didn't comment on the beauty of his words; he had seemed self-conscious last time she had said that. He really had a talent with words, and she wondered if he wrote.

'I can smell snow in the air,' she said. 'That dry, metallic sharpness that always comes before a fall.'

Vivian had worked quietly most of the afternoon, editing the words she had dictated that morning, his soft commentary a companionable murmur as she listened to the audio version of the work they had completed. She let out a satisfied sigh; it was perfect.

They had achieved so much in such a short time; there would be no difficulty making the deadline at his rate. When she called Lila later, she'd be able to tell her how much they'd achieved.

Vivian lingered by the desk, fingertips brushing the stack of old envelopes. "It's strange," he said thoughtfully. "The ink on the letters has faded, but the paper still holds warmth. You can almost feel the emotion left in it."

"Bea always said words hold energy," Dimity replied. "She believed they kept a trace of their maker. Maybe that's why I became a writer—to leave something that lasts beyond me."

He smiled, and she could hear it in his voice. "If that's the measure, you've already succeeded."

She didn't answer, not because she doubted him, but because the compliment struck too close to the ache she carried for everything she'd lost. The sound of the fire filled the quiet instead, a low, living heartbeat. There hadn't been any development in the shapes she'd seen, and the pinprick flashes seemed to have stopped.

As they moved to the fire, Vivian suggested

reading another letter before they stopped for the night. "It feels wrong to leave them unread after so long," he said.

Dimity nodded. "Choose one."

He untied the ribbon again, the faint whisper of parchment filling the room.

My dearest heart, The nights grow longer, and I miss the sound of your laughter in that old cottage. The sergeant says we'll be home by spring. When I close my eyes, I see the orchard in blossom, and I swear I smell your lavender. Keep faith, Bea. Every step I take brings me closer to you.

His voice softened at the last line, and something in it made her throat tighten.

"Arthur was right," she murmured. "The orchard does bloom early here. Every year, even in cold weather."

"Maybe it's waiting," Vivian said quietly.

A log cracked in the fire, sending a scatter of sparks up the chimney. The sound made her start, then laugh at herself.

"I think the cottage approves of your theory," she said.

"Then I'll take that as encouragement."

He replaced the letters carefully, closing the

drawer, and turned towards her. She could sense his movement by the shift in air — the faint rustle of his sleeve, the scent of his cologne mingling with the sweetness of old paper.

'Thank you for letting me read them,' he said. 'They're… unexpectedly moving. He didn't just write about missing her—he wrote about missing this place, these rooms, the garden. As if they were all part of the same love. I can see why you love it here.'

Dimity smiled faintly. 'It's the only place I've ever truly felt at home.'

The silence that followed wasn't awkward. They moved to the kitchen, and their conversation flowed easily as Vivian opened the fridge.

'I think we've eaten all of Mrs Willoughby's meals. There are frozen meals in the freezer if you'd rather,' Dimity offered, trailing her fingers along the counter's edge to orient herself. 'Lila stocked up on what she calls "tragic cardboard cuisine".'

'Absolutely not,' Vivian said, mock-horrified. 'I won't have Mrs Willoughby thinking I'm the sort of man who microwaves his supper. My reputation in the village is at stake.'

She laughed. 'Your reputation? You've been here three days.'

'Exactly. First impressions matter. Now, let's see what we have to work with.' The fridge door opened with a soft suction. 'Eggs, cheese, some rather optimistic-looking vegetables... Right. Omelettes it is.'

'You really can cook, then?' She settled onto one of the kitchen chairs, listening to him move about with confidence as drawers opened and cupboards closed.

'My mother insisted. She said a man who couldn't feed himself was destined for either starvation or a bad marriage.' The crack of eggs against a bowl punctuated his words. 'Mother is an opera singer—dramatic pronouncements are her specialty.'

'An opera singer?' Dimity smiled. 'That explains your voice.'

'Does it?' There was amusement in his tone. 'And here I thought I was just naturally blessed with a pleasing baritone.'

'Naturally blessed and insufferably aware of it, apparently.'

He laughed—a warm, genuine sound that filled the small kitchen. 'My five brothers would agree with you.'

'Five?' She straightened in her chair. 'Good lord, your poor mother.'

'Yes, six boys total. I'm the youngest, which meant I spent my childhood being used as a test subject for various experiments and occasionally as a football.' The whisk clattered against the bowl in a steady rhythm. 'Though it also meant I learned to cook, since I was the only one who'd stay in the kitchen with her. The others were too busy being destructive.'

'It sounds wonderful,' Dimity said softly. 'Chaotic, but wonderful.'

'It was. Is, actually—they're all still speaking to each other, which my mother considers her greatest achievement. My father disagrees. He tries to take the credit.'

'What do they do?' she asked, finding her chair again with only slightly trembling hands. 'Your brothers, I mean. Are they all academics like your father?'

Vivian gave a soft laugh, the tension easing as he plated their food. 'God, no. Dad would have loved that, but we're a disappointingly varied lot.' She heard him set a plate in front of her, the clink of cutlery following.

'Thank you.' She picked up the fork, waiting.

'Right, let's see.' He settled into the chair across from her. 'James is the eldest—he's a barrister in London. Terrifyingly brilliant, argues with everyone, including himself. Then there's Robert, who went into medicine. Cardiac surgeon. Saves lives and has the ego to match.'

'Sounds exhausting,' Dimity said, smiling.

'They are. Then Philip—he's a travel writer, actually. Spends most of his year tramping through places with questionable plumbing and sending back articles about remote villages and extinct languages. We see him every other Christmas if we're lucky.'

'That sounds wonderful,' she said wistfully.

'It does until you remember he once contracted dengue fever and didn't tell anyone for three weeks because he was "documenting the experience".' He paused. 'Andrew's next— he's a marine biologist. Studies coral reefs, rescues turtles, generally makes the rest of us look shallow and self-interested.'

Dimity laughed. 'And the last one?'

'Thomas. He's a chef. Owns a restaurant in Bath—French cuisine, two Michelin stars, absolute torture to eat with because he critiques every meal, including his own.' Vivian's voice warmed with affection. 'He's the only one who understood why I spent my childhood in the kitchen with Mum. The others thought we were mad.'

'Six boys,' Dimity mused. 'Your poor mother.'

'She thrived on it. Still does. Sunday dinners are glorious bedlam—arguments about everything from politics to whether Philip's been properly vaccinated for his latest expedition, someone always stealing food off someone else's plate, and everyone talking over each other because they're too excited to wait their turn—arguing about politics or recipes or whether Philip's latest article was properly sourced.' Warmth surrounded them—the fire crackling in the other room, the soft tick of the clock, two people sharing a meal. Outside, the wind had picked up again, but inside Dimity felt warm and safe.

'Well,' Vivian said at last, 'for what it's worth, I think what you do is extraordinary. And I suspect Bea would have told your mother exactly that.'

Dimity's throat tightened. 'She did, actually.

Several times. Loudly.'

He laughed. 'I like her more and more.'

'She would have liked you too,' Dimity said, then felt her cheeks warm at the admission.

Another comfortable silence. Then Vivian cleared his throat. 'Right. Pudding. I saw some rather lonely-looking apples in the fruit bowl. Apple crumble?'

'You're going to spoil me,' she warned.

'Perhaps that's the plan,' he said lightly. But something in his tone made her pulse quicken.

She heard him stand, collecting their plates. As he passed behind her chair, his hand brushed her shoulder—brief, possibly accidental, but it sent a pleasant shiver cascading down her spine.

The cottage gave a contented creak, a floorboard settling as if in approval.

'I heard that,' Vivian said to the room at large.

Dimity smiled. 'It's pleased with you.'

'Is it, now?'

'Very. You passed the cooking test. That's important in this house.'

'And what happens if I pass all the tests?' he asked, his voice closer than she expected. He must have stopped behind her chair.

Her breath caught. 'I suppose we'll have to wait and see.'

Her pulse kicked against her ribs. Vivian was still standing there, close enough that she could feel his warmth. Then he moved away, back to the counter, and she could breathe again. But the warmth lingered.

'Apple crumble it is, then,' he said. 'Consider it practice for test number two.'

'What's test number two?'

'I'll let you know when I figure it out.'

She laughed, and the sound filled the kitchen like light.

'What about you? Any siblings?'

'Two older sisters.' She traced the wood grain of the table with her fingertip. 'Both of whom have pleased Mum enormously by marrying nice, sensible men and producing a steady stream of grandchildren.'

'And you're the misfit,' he said, not unkindly.

'The misfit,' she confirmed. 'The one who writes "fantasy nonsense" and lives in a cottage overseas instead of getting a real job.'

'A real job,' he repeated, and she could hear the smile in his voice. 'By which she means something that doesn't involve magic, romance, or believing in things that can't be quantified?'

'Precisely.'

'Well, clearly your mother hasn't read your sales figures.' The sound of butter sizzling in a pan drifted across the kitchen. 'Or perhaps she has, and is simply terrified you might actually succeed.'

Dimity blinked, surprised by the observation. 'That's... remarkably perceptive, but no, she hasn't. She thinks I'm supporting myself waitressing.'

'I have five brothers, remember? I know complicated family dynamics.' He paused. 'Can you reach the plates in the cupboard above you? Second shelf.'

She stood carefully, counting her steps, then reached up. Her fingers found the cupboard handle, pulled it open. 'How many?'

'Two should do. Unless you're planning to eat like my brother Thomas, in which case we'll need four.'

She laughed, reaching for the plates. But as she pulled them down, something shifted—the cupboard door swung wider than she'd opened it, catching her off-balance. She stumbled back just as the overhead shelf groaned ominously.

'Dimity—' Vivian's voice, sharp with concern.

Then his hands were on her waist, steadying her, pulling her back from the cupboard as a cascade of books tumbled down—old, heavy volumes that Bea must have stored there with recipes decades ago. They hit the counter with a series of solid thumps, right where Dimity had been standing.

For a moment, neither of them moved. His hands were still at her waist, her back pressed against his chest. She could feel his heart beating—quick, startled—and the warmth of his breath near her temple.

'Are you all right?' he asked quietly.

'Yes.' Her voice came out smaller than intended. 'Yes, I'm fine. Thank you.'

But neither of them stepped away. The kitchen had gone very still around them—even the pan had stopped its sizzling, as if the cottage itself was holding its breath. Waiting…

'That was...' He trailed off.

'The cottage,' she finished. 'I told you it meddles.'

'Quite effectively, apparently.' His voice was

low, edged with something she couldn't quite name. His hands hadn't moved from her waist.

She should step away. Should laugh it off. Should do anything other than remain exactly where she was, feeling the solid warmth of him at her back, the kitchen suddenly too small for two people.

'Vivian,' she said softly.

'Yes?' His head moved closer to hers; she could feel the warmth of his breath.

'The apple's burning.'

He swore and released her, turning quickly to the stove. The spell broke, but the warmth remained, humming in the space between them as he rescued their pudding and she stood, pulse racing, fingers pressed to the counter where his hands had been.

Behind them, the cupboard door swung gently closed with a satisfied click.

'Well,' Vivian said after a moment, his voice not quite steady, 'at least we know the cottage approves of apple crumble.'

Dimity laughed, shaky but genuine. 'Among other things.'

He didn't answer, but she knew he'd been smiling. If only she could see it. If she could see his eyes, she'd know if what she had felt between them was reciprocated.

They settled by the fire with their pudding, the warmth from the flames reaching across the room. Dimity savoured the apple, the tartness melting on her tongue.

'This is divine,' she said. 'Thank you for making it. You really can cook.'

'My pleasure.'

They ate in comfortable silence for a moment, then she felt him lean closer. 'May I?' His voice was soft, careful.

'I—yes?'

The briefest touch of linen against her lips, his fingers steady and gentle. 'A spot of cream,' he said quietly, and she heard the smile in his voice.

She refused to feel embarrassed. 'Oh. Thank you.'

'Goodnight, Dimity,' he said a while later, his voice warm. 'Sleep well.'

'Goodnight, Vivian.'

She listened to his footsteps fade, then sat for a long moment in the firelight's warmth. Was he simply being kind? Considerate? Or had there been something in that gentle touch that meant more?

She really liked this man—liked the steadiness she sensed in him, the thoughtfulness in his voice, the care in his movements. She didn't need to see him to know she was drawn to him in a way that both thrilled and unnerved her. The question was whether he felt even a fraction of what she did.

After he wished her goodnight and left the study, Dimity lingered, fingers tracing the edge of the desk.

Then, just as she turned to leave, something shifted—a flicker behind her eyelids, faint but undeniable.

Light.

She gasped softly. It wasn't shape or detail, but colour—warm, golden, pulsing like candlelight through water. She stood perfectly still, afraid that moving would break the spell.

And then the room appeared shimmering before her; the pink rose wallpaper, the deep amber glow of the fire reflected in the window glass, the rich burgundy of the armchair's velvet. Colours she remembered but hadn't dared hope to see again. They swam together, blurred but unmistakable—alive.

Her hand flew to her mouth, pressing against the sob that threatened to escape. The desk materialised in soft browns and golds, Arthur's letters a pale cream against the dark wood. The bookshelf emerged from shadow, spine after familiar spine—reds, greens, the faded blue of Bea's favourite poetry collection.

It lasted perhaps ten seconds. Then, like a setting sun, the colours faded—first the wallpaper, then the books, the fire dimming to an orange ghost before disappearing entirely. The darkness returned, but softer now, as if it had lost some of its harshness.

She stood trembling, one hand gripping the edge of the desk, the other still pressed to her lips. Tears spilled hot down her cheeks.

'It's coming back,' she whispered to the empty room. 'Oh God, it's coming back.'

Her legs gave way. She sank into the armchair, buried her face in her hands, and wept—not from grief this time, but with hope so fierce it took her breath away.

Her reaction eased slowly, leaving her heart thudding, her palms damp. For a long moment, she stayed there, breathing in the scent of wood polish and faint smoke, and the comfort of knowing that Vivian was upstairs.

It's coming back, she thought. *I'm seeing.*

She wasn't going to share. Not yet. Not until she was sure it was coming back.

Dimity stood and moved towards the doorway, her hand finding the frame, and smiled into the dark.

'Thank you, Bea,' she whispered. 'And you too, Pippin's Nook.'

Somewhere behind her, a single page of Arthur's letter lifted and fell as if stirred by a sigh.

Chapter Ten

The snow came just after dawn.

Dimity woke with her heart already racing, the memory of last night flooding back before she was fully conscious. *Colours. I saw colours.*

She lay perfectly still, almost afraid to breathe. Her hand moved to her face, fingers trembling as they hovered near her closed eyelids. What if it had been a dream? A cruel trick of exhausted nerves and wishful thinking?

The world was muffled in stillness as she climbed out of bed and made her way to the window. The faint chill of the glass met her fingers as she reached for the curtain, the light beyond soft and diffused. She drew a slow breath and opened her eyes.

Darkness. But not complete. Not the absolute black she'd grown accustomed to.

She blinked, concentrating. There—was that a lighter patch where the glass was? A suggestion of grey against black? She turned her head towards where she knew the curtains hung, and yes, there was definitely something. Not shape, not detail, but a softness in the darkness, like charcoal smudged on paper.

A sob caught in her throat—half disappointment that the vivid colours hadn't returned, half wonder that anything remained at all. She took a deep breath and reached out to the chest of drawers where Lila had organised her clothes. Underwear, clean jeans, and a long-sleeved T-shirt.

Downstairs, she could hear Vivian moving about—the kettle clicking on, the scrape of a chair, the low thud of logs added to the fire.

'Good morning,' he called lightly up the stairwell. 'We appear to be snowed in.'

She smiled. 'How bad?'

'Bad enough that the lane's disappeared entirely. Picturesque, provided one ignores the fact that we can't get out in an emergency.'

'I imagine we'll survive,' she said, pulling on her T-shirt.

By the time she reached the kitchen, the fire was glowing and the scent of coffee filled the air. Vivian's voice came from near the window, describing the scene for her.

'The orchard's white right through to the stone wall. The branches look like lacework. It's really quite beautiful.'

'You're good at this—narration,' she said, leaning against the table.

He laughed. 'An occupational hazard. It helps me picture what an author's trying to achieve.'

'It's working. I can see it perfectly.'

They shared breakfast and a second coffee before settling in the study. Fire crackling, Vivian opened his notes.

'Chapter twenty-two,' he said. 'Elara and the fae court.'

He began to read, his voice wrapping around the words she'd written here alone, months ago. Hearing her prose read in his beautiful voice brought it alive for her.

She was disappointed when he broke off to comment, suggesting a rearrangement of paragraphs. 'That way it lets the reader imagine what's going to happen, and then the unexpected comes. "*The fae lord spoke, and the storm obeyed" at the end of the paragraph.*'

Simple, stronger. She nodded. 'Yes. Better.'

'I'm just trimming the brush so the light reaches the path,' he said.

She smiled at his metaphor.

They worked until a firm knock broke the

rhythm.

'Mrs Willoughby,' Dimity guessed.

Vivian opened the door to a gust of cold air and a bustle of good cheer. 'Soup and scones for the stranded!' their neighbour announced. 'Trapped up here like characters in one of those BBC dramas.'

Dimity laughed. 'You shouldn't have come out in this.'

'Nonsense. Bea's house has always looked after its people,' Mrs Willoughby said knowingly. 'And you, young man—keep our Dimity fed. Last time she had a deadline, Bea told me she forgot to eat for two days.'

'I'll do my best,' Vivian replied.

As she left, the old kitchen door stuck. Dimity and Vivian leaned together until it gave way, laughter spilling between them.

'See?' she said breathlessly. 'The house conspires.'

'A mischievous one,' he agreed. 'But I can't say I mind.'

When the door finally closed, warmth between them lingered.

The storm intensified through the afternoon,

snow piling on the sills until the world vanished. Dimity loved the way Vivian described the changes in the landscape as the day passed. Inside, firelight and the tap of keys filled the quiet. She dictated; he typed, reading back each line so she could hear the cadence.

'"*The battle raged, and through the roar of wind and flame, Elara heard his voice—steady, calling her name*".'

'That's lovely,' he said. 'It echoes her earlier hesitation.'

'You hear things I don't remember doing.'

'Your writing is instinctive. That's the best kind to edit—discovering what's already there.'

Evening came early. The power flickered once before steadying. He brought her tea, and for a while they sat in contented silence.

When a log split with a sudden crack, she smiled. 'It does that sometimes—lights itself when the room grows too cold.'

'Convenient magic,' he said.

'Bea would call it the house lending a hand.'

He hesitated. 'You really do believe that?'

'I'm not sure what I believe,' she said softly. 'Only that it feels alive here—as if it remembers.'

'Then perhaps it's remembering her happy memories,' he murmured, 'and trying to create new ones.'

Her breath caught. The fire hissed softly, and the cottage seemed to sigh.

##

Night settled, and the snow kept falling. They'd moved to the sitting room, tea steaming between them.

'May I ask you something?' Vivian said, his voice quieter now.

'You may.'

'Why fantasy? You write it like someone who believes it can save a life.'

'It saved mine,' she said. 'When I was small, I was always the odd one out. And then at school, the same. Stories made space where there wasn't any. And now… they lead me through life, if that makes sense.'

He didn't rush to fill the pause. She liked that about him.

'I tried writing once,' he said finally. 'A sprawling epic—three maps, seven invented languages. The hard drive died at sixty thousand words. I told myself it was mercy.'

'Do you miss it?'

'Sometimes. When I read something like Elara on the ridge, I feel the ache of not having tried harder. I feel as though I've failed.'

'Then maybe that's your path still,' she said. 'You already know how to find the light.'

He laughed softly. 'Careful. That sounds like encouragement.'

'Take it as a professional hazard.'

They smiled in the firelight. Dimity's fingers found Aunt Bea's carved bird on the mantel; the smooth curve steadied her.

'Since we're confessing,' she said quietly, 'I've always felt inadequate. Like I was fumbling through life without a plan while everyone else seemed to know exactly where they were going.'

'And now?' His voice was gentle, attentive.

'Now I've written something people want to read, and I'm terrified.' She gave a shaky laugh. 'Terrified I'll change. That success will turn me into someone I don't recognise. Someone who forgets where she came from, or worse—someone who believes she deserves it and becomes insufferable.'

Vivian was quiet for a moment. 'Do you want to know what I think?'

'Please.'

'I think the people who worry about changing for the worse rarely do. It's the ones who never question themselves you have to watch.' His voice warmed. 'And from what I've seen, you're far too self-aware to lose yourself. Success doesn't change who we are—it just reveals us more clearly.'

Her throat tightened. 'That's either very comforting or terrifying.'

'Both, probably,' he said, and she could hear the smile in his voice. 'But I'd bet on you, Dimity. You've already walked through darkness and found your way back to words. That takes more courage than most people have.'

'Thank you,' she whispered.

'Besides,' he added, lighter now, 'anyone who names a character Elara and gives her a backbone made of steel is going to be just fine.'

She laughed, the tension breaking. 'Spoken like a man haunted by seven invented languages.'

'I don't know who you were before,' he said gently, 'but I'm pretty sure you are still the same person.'

Her throat tightened. 'Thank you.'

##

Later, they turned back to the manuscript.

'One last pass?' he suggested. 'The scene where Elara asks him to stay.'

'If you'll catch me when I fall.'

'I'm here,' he said simply.

She dictated the scene that was in her head: 'If I ask you to stay, it isn't kindness I want. Not rescue. I want the fierce part—the part that argues, that stands beside me when it's hard.'

He read it back, and her pulse raced.

'Good?' he asked.

'Good,' she managed.

He continued until the scene reached its climax—a kiss not yet taken.

'Shall we stop there?' he asked softly.

'Yes,' she said, though she meant not yet.

The lights flickered, the fire flared as if in answer. In the kitchen, the kettle clicked on by itself. Vivian laughed under his breath. 'Convenient magic indeed.'

'Bea would call it good manners,' Dimity murmured. 'The house doesn't like to end a day on a half-finished sentence.'

'Shall we have a cup of tea?'

They rose together. The kitchen door stuck again as Vivian turned the knob; their shoulders brushed as they leaned, the latch yielding slowly. Steam curled from the kettle—filled perfectly, though neither recalled filling it.

He poured the tea. She listened to the familiar sounds: spoon on china, fire hush, winter pressing against the glass.

'Thank you for today,' she said.

'Thank you for trusting me,' he replied. 'For letting me carry the words awhile.'

At the foot of the stairs, Dimity paused. 'Goodnight, Vivian.'

'Goodnight, Dimity.' A quiet beat. 'We're close to something—on the page, I mean. I can feel it.'

'So can I.'

She climbed, counting the steps she knew by heart. From below came the soft rustle of a page.

'Goodnight, Bea,' she whispered.

And for an instant, gold light flared behind her eyes—as if someone had lifted a lantern at the end of the hall. It faded, but the warmth remained, wrapping her in contentment.

Downstairs, the fire burned steadily, and the house seemed to settle.

Writer and editor, cottage and snow—all waiting for morning.

Chapter Eleven

Dimity woke with a start, aware of light before she remembered why that mattered. She lay very still, eyes closed, letting the brightness rest against her lids. When she opened them, there was nothing at first—then a pulse of pale gold where the window ought to be, a darker band that might be the wardrobe. Shapes. Not invented by her mind. Real.

She didn't move. Maybe it was time to call Dr Hughes. It was still a week until the car would come to take her to London.

Downstairs, the kettle began its loud whistle. She smiled, the daily routine pleasing her. Vivian's footsteps crossed the kitchen; a cupboard opened, closed, and the clinking of crockery accompanied her as she dressed.

'Good morning,' he called gently up the stairs. 'The world appears less treacherous today. I can see patches of blue.'

After using the bathroom and scrubbing her face with a flannel, she made her way downstairs, counting the steps with the banister under her palm.

Vivian was by the window. He was a deeper shape against a brighter one—movement where once there had been only sound. She didn't let herself look too hard.

'You're cheerful,' she said.

'Breakfast does that to a man,' he replied. 'Also, the prospect of revising a chapter where a minor character attempts to overthrow a fae tribunal. I do love a doomed coup.'

They ate toast and apricot jam, and then the work began. The study warmed around them as Vivian read from her draft, and the morning took on the familiar rhythm—his voice, her corrections, the faint scratch of his pen.

Elara stood at the edge of the frost forest and listened to the trees argue quietly in the wind. Behind her, the night-lanterns guttered; before her, the snow caught the dawn like milk poured over glass. She drew the hood closer, wishing for the warmth of a hand that wasn't there.

Vivian paused. 'You give the snow a texture you can taste,' he said. 'Lovely.'

'Keep going,' she murmured.

When the first arrow fell, it hissed, and the sound broke her indecision. She ran, the cold snapping at her ankles like a thing with teeth, until a voice—his voice—cut the world in two. 'This way.'

Dimity pressed her fingers together in her lap, surprised by the prickle behind her eyes. 'Read that again,' she said. 'From "the snow caught the dawn". But slower.'

He did, and as he spoke, she felt the next scene arrive inside her like magic. She lifted her eyes. For the first time since the accident, she wasn't just hearing her world—she was seeing its outline. A pale wash where a window must be. The darker suggestion of the desk. If she turned her head, the fire was a living thing— dimmer, then brighter.

She swallowed, careful not to let any of it onto her face. Not yet.

By late morning, another two chapters complete, and their momentum was interrupted by a brisk knock and a cheerful gust of wind. Mrs Willoughby swept in, parcels in both arms, a flurry of cold air and cinnamon.

'Darlings,' she announced, 'the village market is today. They've put the stalls around the church and strung lights from lamppost to lamppost—very pretty. I've brought mincemeat and a scandalous amount of clotted cream. Oh, and scones.' She deposited her parcels, patted Dimity's hand, and lowered her voice to a mock whisper. 'You'll go to the market, won't you? The brass band at six, carols at half past. It's practically the law.'

'We have three chapters to finish,' Dimity began, but Mrs Willoughby had already moved on; milk, bread, the rumour of a storm tomorrow. Before she left, she added, almost as an afterthought, 'Pippin's Nook likes an outing. It did Bea good to get into the village, even when Arthur was away. Don't let the cottage down.'

When the door thudded shut, Vivian chuckled. 'It appears we've been instructed.'

'She's formidable,' Dimity said fondly.

'True. And right.'

He hesitated before he replied. 'Would you like to go? I can—if you'd like—be your eyes for the evening.'

'Yes,' she said, surprising herself. 'I would.'

They worked until the light thinned. When it was time, Vivian helped her with her coat. She decided to take her cane but also his arm, her hand settling just above his elbow, where his sleeve was warm and faintly textured. She resisted running her fingers along the wool. Outside, the air was cold enough to make breathing sharp; the lane held their footsteps like a secret.

'Mind the ridge,' he warned gently, guiding her around ice that her feet couldn't read fast enough. He described their walk without fuss—the hedgerows laced with frost, the blackbirds punting along the hedge tops, the way the sky blushed near the horizon.

'It looks like the world's waiting,' he said. 'And the church tower's wearing a very silly hat of snow.'

They reached the village to bells and chatter, the laughter of children, the resin-thick scent of pine. They stepped under the garlands, and Vivian described where they were. Stalls with striped awnings. Jars of amber honey catching light. Ropes of dried orange slices like small suns. Strangers who weren't quite strangers when they said 'Evening, Dimity,' and 'Good to have you back, love.'

She absorbed his words and let them paint her world. But sometimes they didn't have to. Sometimes her eyes gave her a gift—a flicker, a suggestion. Light pooling on cobbles. The dark tree shape against a lantern, crowned by a small, trembling star. She said nothing, hoarding each fragment with hope.

'Hot mulled cider?' Vivian asked.

'Yes, please.' The paper cup warmed her hands as she inhaled the smell of cloves. A brass band attempted 'God Rest Ye Merry, Gentlemen' with more cheer than accuracy. Somewhere, a dog shook, tags clinking like tiny bells.

'Tell me the colours,' she said.

'Gold and green mostly,' he answered. 'But the particular gold of lamplight on frost. The particular green of garlands when the needles catch it. Your scarf is a deep red that behaves very well with winter.'

'Behaves well,' she repeated, amused.

'Do you want ornaments for the tree?' Vivian asked.

Dimity paused. 'What tree?'

'The one in the front room. By the window.'

She frowned. 'There's a tree in the front room?'

'A Christmas tree, yes. A rather nice fir, actually. It must have been there when you arrived.'

'Lila didn't mention a tree.' Dimity's frown deepened. 'She told me about every tactile marker, every potential hazard, every piece of furniture. She wouldn't have forgotten to mention a six-foot tree in the middle of the room.'

'Well, it's there now.' Vivian sounded bemused. 'Though I have to admit, I didn't notice it until today.'

'You didn't notice it?'

'I know how that sounds, but no. I've been in that room a dozen times, and today—there it was. Perfectly placed, as if it had always been there.'

They were both quiet for a moment.

'Aunt Bea,' they said in unison.

Dimity shook her head slowly, half smiling. 'Of course it was.'

'Does she do this often?' Vivian asked carefully. 'Rearrange things? Appear... trees?'

'I'm beginning to think she does whatever she pleases,' Dimity said. 'And apparently, she's decided we need a Christmas tree.'

They bought a small box of glass ornaments for the Christmas tree in the front room from a woman who reverently pronounced "baubles" as though offering Waterford Crystal. Mrs

Willoughby appeared from nowhere to press a sprig of mistletoe into Dimity's hand with a wicked grin. 'For the front room,' she said. 'A tree that appears on its own deserves proper trimming.'

Dimity stilled. 'How did you know—'

'Bea's cottage has always had a mind of its own, dear. They'll do in our village.' Mrs Willoughby patted her hand and hurried away.

They stayed for the carols. Vivian sang softly, his voice easy among the crowd, coaxing her into the melody. When the final note thinned into night, he bent his head to speak near her ear, and for a moment she felt the warmth of his breath against her hair. It made her heart ache with want, the sort of feeling she had given to Elara many times.

They walked home slowly, and the cottage welcomed them with its familiar theatrics—the latch that yielded at first touch, the sigh of warm air from the hall, a log catching perfectly as if coaxed.

'Tea?' he asked.

'In a minute,' she said. 'Let's do the decorations first.'

They stood close to the tree—an old ceramic

pot with a pine that had opinions of its own. Vivian described the branches, and Dimity hung the glass shapes where he guided her—an apple that glowed like a hearth when the firelight found it, a star that chimed faintly as if convinced it was crystal. She reached into the box for another ornament, and their fingers touched, warm skin to warm skin.

'Sorry,' he said, a breath late.

'Don't be,' she managed.

They hung the mistletoe last. She lifted it, and he stepped behind her to tie it to the kitchen lintel. The old door, which had stuck all week, swung obligingly open to accommodate his reach, then closed with a satisfied little click. Dimity didn't comment.

They made tea, and at the table, Vivian opened his notebook. 'We did good work today,' he said. 'Tomorrow, let's look at the tribunal sequence again. There's a line there that wants a sharper knife.'

Dimity smiled. 'Read me the latest notes?'

He began, and after a page, he slipped into her text—the scene she'd dictated that morning.

Elara lifted the latch. The wind pressed in as if eager to be invited, bringing the scent of iron and pine. 'If I ask you to stay,' she said, 'I need you to understand it isn't kindness I want from you. It isn't a rescue. I want the fierce part—the part that argues with me when I'm wrong, and stands beside me when I'm right, and refuses to look away when it's difficult.'

Vivian's voice gentled even more on the last clause. He didn't embellish the moment. He let it stand.

Dimity cleared her throat. 'Add—' And I want to be that for you.' Short sentence. Simple.'

He wrote. 'Done.'

They worked another hour, small refinements and quiet laughter. When the clock on the mantel chimed nine, they stopped as if the cottage had made the decision for them.

'Thank you,' she said when they reached the stairs. 'For… describing the market. I could see it.'

'Thank you for trusting me to,' he said, and she could hear the smile in his voice.

At the first step, she looked towards the sitting room. The fire had found its slow glow. The tree hummed faintly with its delicate glass. And—yes—she could just make out a tall, darker shape turning towards the kitchen: Vivian, a broad shape in the lamplight, solid and gentle and there.

'I'll bank the fire,' he said behind her.

She nodded, afraid her voice would give away too much. 'Goodnight, Vivian.'

'Goodnight, Dimity.'

She climbed carefully. At the landing, she paused and turned back. The house breathed around her—warm timber, lavender ghosts, the cold of winter waiting beyond the glass. She let her eyes rest and saw the barest outline: doorway, banister, the softer rectangle of the window beyond. Not fantasy. Not imagined. There.

In her room, she sat on the edge of the bed and pressed her palms together until the tremor eased.

Two truths presented themselves with the steadiness of facts:

Her sight was returning—slowly, shyly, like a heart learning to hope again.

And she was falling in love with the sound of a man who made her words feel like home.

Downstairs, the cottage agreed—a candle on the mantel gave a soft, unquestionable pop and bloomed into flame. The scent of vanilla drifted through the hall as if someone had opened a tin of biscuits in another century.

'Bea,' Dimity whispered, smiling into the dark, 'behave.'

The cottage made no promises. It merely went on holding them in its keeping—writer and editor, steady voice and returning sight—while snow settled on the orchard wall and the star in the market square watched over the village.

Chapter Twelve

The storm had eased overnight, but the world still felt wrapped in its hush. A pale wash of morning light spilled across the snowdrifts outside, and the cottage breathed in its quiet rhythm — the tick of the clock, the soft groan of timber, the hiss of the Aga warming again.

Dimity lingered at the top of the stairs, listening. Below, Vivian's voice carried—low, measured, and unfamiliar in tone.

'Yes, I understand, but that's not the situation. She's my client.' A pause. Then, more tightly, 'No, of course not. It's professional. Entirely professional.'

The floorboard beneath her foot creaked; the conversation stopped. A few moments later, the kettle clicked, and his tone returned to the calm she knew.

When she entered the kitchen, Vivian greeted her. 'Good morning. The agency sends its blessings, and a list of new forms to complete, naturally.'

Dimity didn't reply. Her heart was thudding.

She could hear what he wasn't saying, but her attention was focused on the faint shimmer of shadow when he moved across the room towards her. It wasn't the sound; she could see where he was moving.

##

They began work soon after breakfast. The fire crackled in the grate, and a tremor of wind whispered beneath the eaves. The study had grown to feel like an extension of them both — notebooks stacked neatly at Vivian's elbow, her dictation recorder waiting beside a cooling cup of tea.

'Where were we?' she asked.

'Chapter twenty-seven,' he said, his tone softening as he found the place. 'Elara's confession.'

Dimity nodded. 'Right. Let's get it over with.'

He began to read, and the air shifted between them.

'*She could no longer tell where her magic ended and his began. His voice found her through the dark, steady as a tide, and the walls she had built through a lifetime of battle began to fall, one by one.*'

He paused, clearing his throat. 'Lovely metaphor. Perhaps "one by one" could go. The rhythm stands without it.'

'Agreed,' she said quickly, her voice steadier than her pulse.

He continued.

'He stepped closer, every heartbeat of distance closing until there was only breath, and then even that was shared.'

The silence that followed felt alive. The scratch of his pen, the shift of his sleeve—every small sound was as intimate as touch.

'Do you want to hear it aloud again?' he asked quietly.

She almost said no. Instead: 'Yes.'

He did, and this time she heard something different—not just her words, but the catch in his breathing, the way certain lines seemed to cost him something to speak aloud.

When he finished, neither spoke.

It was Vivian who broke the spell first, standing abruptly. 'I think we need to take a break.'

'Good idea,' she whispered, her hands trembling in her lap. Had she imagined the shift in his voice? The yearning behind those words?

Or was he feeling this too—this dangerous pull neither of them could name?

Chapter Thirteen

Outside, the snow gleamed wet and bright in the early December sun. Vivian fetched firewood from the shed, intent on what he was doing; anything to stop thinking about Dimity.

Professional. Controlled. Inside, he was unravelling.

Every word he'd read had mirrored his feelings; the lines she'd written about trust, surrender, the courage to want… they had struck deeper than any edit should.

He stacked the logs too neatly, his hands shaking faintly from more than cold. *I'm being unprofessional. She trusts me. Don't ruin this.*

When he came back inside with some of the firewood, Dimity was standing by the window, face turned towards the light.

'Are you all right?' he asked.

She smiled, but it was gone as quickly as it came. 'I think so.'

##

That afternoon, Mrs Willoughby arrived with another armful of groceries and her usual cheery disposition.

'I swear the whole village's talking about you two,' she said, setting down a bag of apples. 'All that light shining from this place at night. It looks like a fairy tale in there. You'll have people thinking Pippin's Nook is matchmaking again.'

Dimity laughed nervously. Vivian said, 'We're simply working late.'

'Of course you are, dear,' Mrs Willoughby said, her eyes twinkling. 'That's what Bea said the first winter Arthur stayed here, too.'

They were both tired by early evening. Vivian sat at the desk, reading through the printout of Dimity's dictation. She'd written Elara's climactic battle, where love and magic became the same.

'The power rose through her like fire, wild and terrifying and right. When she spoke his name, the world stilled to listen.'

He looked up. 'You've found it again. The perfect cadence.'

Her cheeks warmed. 'It feels different now. The story's writing itself.'

'Or as if something's helping,' he said with a faint smile, glancing towards the flickering fire.

When they finished for the night, the cottage

felt different—intense, the air between them charged with something he didn't dare examine too closely.

He stood, needing space, needing air. 'Would you like to take a walk? In the garden?'

'A walk?'

'Just to stretch our legs,' he added quickly. Too quickly. 'We've been sitting for hours. The fresh air might do us good.'

'It's dark out.'

'I know. I'll guide you. If you'd like.' He hesitated. 'We don't have to.'

She smiled. 'No, a walk sounds lovely. I'd like that.'

Relief flooded through him, though he wasn't entirely sure what he was relieved about—that she'd said yes, or that he'd have a reason to step outside these walls that suddenly felt far too intimate.

'Let me get your coat,' he said.

***

The air outside was crisp, redolent with woodsmoke and apple bark. Vivian stood on the small porch beside Dimity, suddenly aware of how close they were standing.

'The snow's lying across the garden in a

smooth white quilt,' he said quietly. 'The moon's climbed above the orchard—pale and perfect.'

'Thank you.' She smiled. 'Beautiful words. I can see it.'

She hesitated at the door, then stepped forward without reaching for her cane. His chest tightened at the trust in that gesture.

'I'll guide you,' he said, though she didn't seem to need it. Instead, he found himself painting the world for her, unable to stop the words. 'The snow's crusted with silver—catches the moonlight like powdered glass. The birdbath's frozen over, a perfect disk. And the orchard...' He paused, looking at the skeletal branches. 'Each branch looks sculpted. The roses on the trellis are just shadows, but they look as if they're waiting for spring.'

She was smiling, and his heart ached at the sight.

'You should write again,' she said.

He chuckled, though it came out rougher than he'd intended. 'Editing's safer. Other people's dreams are easier to fix than your own.'

They stopped beneath the apple trees, the old branches arching above them like a cathedral. She breathed in deeply, and he watched her face transform—peaceful, present, beautiful in the moonlight.

'It is beautiful,' she murmured. 'I can almost see it.'

He turned towards her fully then, unable to help himself. 'Then you're seeing it exactly right.'

A gust of wind shook the branches, scattering flakes that caught in her dark hair, glittering like stars. He reached out before he could think better of it, his fingers gentle as he brushed them away.

'You've got snow on you,' he said softly, his voice betraying him. 'And the moon's doing you favours.'

She laughed, breathless and shy. 'You shouldn't say things like that.'

'I know.' He meant it as an apology, but it came out as a confession. 'But I might anyway.'

For a moment, they stood there, the orchard silent around them, and he was acutely aware of every inch of space between them—how easy it would be to close it, how impossible it felt to move away.

He forced himself to step back. 'We should go in. It's getting colder. You don't want to catch a chill.'

'Yes,' she said, and he couldn't tell if that was relief or disappointment in her voice.

They walked towards the cottage, its windows glowing gold against the silver snow, woodsmoke curling from the chimney. He kept his hands carefully at his sides, resisting the urge to take her arm, to touch her again, to do any of the dozen things he suddenly, desperately wanted.

That night, Vivian couldn't sleep. He lay awake replaying every moment in the garden—the snow in her hair, the way Dimity had smiled, how close he'd come to forgetting every professional boundary he'd ever had.

A soft creak from downstairs made him still. Then another. Footsteps—Dimity's, light and barefoot in the hall.

He rose, pulling on his shirt, and stepped into the corridor and turned the light on.

Was he dreaming or had the cottage gone mad?

Mistletoe hung from every lintel and beam—not one or two sprigs, but dozens of them, appearing where none had been before. Fresh, green, glistening. The air smelled sharply of apples and pine.

In the kitchen doorway, Dimity stood laughing softly, shaking her head. 'Oh, Bea. Really?'

'Dimity?' His voice came out rougher than he'd intended.

She turned towards him, and something in her expression made him stop breathing.

'Nothing's wrong,' she said, smiling in a way that suggested everything was about to change. 'The house is just… meddling.'

He stepped into the lamplight, suddenly self-conscious—hair rumpled, shirt half-buttoned, caught somewhere between sleep and waking. Her eyes tracked over him, and for a heartbeat, he could have sworn she could see him—truly see him.

The thought made his pulse stutter.

Neither of them spoke.

Above them, the mistletoe trembled slightly, as if caught in an invisible breeze—or as if the cottage itself was laughing.

Chapter Fourteen

Morning crept in, as if the cottage was holding its breath. The snow had stopped sometime in the night, and pale sunlight pooled across the floorboards in wavering shapes.

Dimity stood by the window, one hand resting lightly on the frame. She could see the light now—not just feel its warmth, but the faint, living movement of it. The world had colour again. Bleached gold, muted blue. The outline of trees. The shimmer of frost on the orchard wall.

She bit her lip to keep from smiling. Joy fluttered behind her ribs, fragile and giddy. Then, almost at once, came guilt.

If she told Vivian, what then?

He would leave—duty-bound, professional to the end. The thought was unbearable.

She pressed her fingers to the windowpane, the cold anchoring her. *Not yet*, she thought. *Let me have this joy just a little longer.*

She smiled as she chose her favourite shirt, red for Christmas.

Vivian was already in the kitchen, sleeves

rolled to his forearms, the scent of toast and marmalade warming the air. He looked up as she entered.

'Good morning,' he said, his smile gentle but tired. 'Did you sleep?'

'Eventually,' she lied. 'And you?'

'Barely.' He poured her tea, the spoon clinking softly against the cup. 'I kept hearing odd noises. Did you notice… the mistletoe?'

Dimity forced a casual tone. 'I did. The cottage has a sense of humour.'

'So it seems.' His voice was dry, but there was amusement beneath it. 'You should see it now. It's as if the ceiling's been redecorated by a romantic ghost.'

She laughed, but the sound caught somewhere in her throat. 'We'll leave it for now. Bea would approve.'

He studied her for a moment, the warmth in his expression tempered by something quieter— uncertainty, perhaps. 'About last night…'

'Yes?'

He hesitated. 'Nothing happened. But it might have. And that complicates things.'

Dimity lowered her cup. 'Does it?'

'Of course it does,' he said softly. 'I'm here

in a professional capacity. You're my client. The agency is already nervous about my… unconventional methods. Living in the cottage with you.' He smiled wryly, but the humour didn't reach his eyes. 'I'm rather fond of this job. I'd hate to give them reason to think I've lost objectivity.'

You haven't lost it, she wanted to say. You've just found your heart again.

Instead, she nodded. 'Understood.'

They worked through the morning, words a little more deliberate than usual. The air between them held a new awkwardness.

When Vivian read aloud, his voice was as beautiful as before—but she could hear the caution, the change that lay beneath. She had been kidding herself and likening him to Lord Ashton in her imagination.

Chapter Fifteen

The first weeks of December slipped by like pages turning in a well-loved book—each day bringing Dimity and Vivian closer to the end of the manuscript, and closer to something neither of them had acknowledged.

The life together—as writer and editor—had settled into a rhythm. Breakfast and coffee together, hours of work punctuated by Vivian's careful readings and thoughtful edits. Lunch by the fire. Afternoon edits. Evening walks in the garden when the weather allowed, or quiet conversations over tea when it didn't.

And through it all, Dimity's vision continued its slow, miraculous return.

She could see shapes now—clear, defined shapes. The outline of Vivian as he moved around the kitchen. The glow of lamplight against the walls. The red and gold spines of books on Aunt Bea's shelves. Each day brought more detail, more colour, more of the world back into focus.

She told no one.

##

The appointment with Dr Hughes came on a grey Tuesday. Lila had booked her transport, and it was strange to leave the cottage. Vivian was worried as he saw her off.

'Are you sure you don't want me to come?'

'No, there is work to do here. We're running out of time.'

Dr Hughes was delighted.

'Sixty percent,' he said, his voice full of satisfaction. 'Sixty percent, Dimity. This is extraordinary. I've never seen anything quite like it.' He shone his light, made his notations, and asked her to read progressively smaller letters on the chart. 'Remarkable. Truly remarkable.'

'What does this mean?' she asked carefully. 'Long term?'

'It's hard to say with certainty, but given the trajectory of your recovery...' He paused, choosing his words. 'I would say there's every reason to hope for near-complete restoration in the very near future. Perhaps not perfect vision—you may always need reading glasses, for instance—but functional, independent sight.'

Independent.

The word should have filled her with joy.

Instead, it settled like a stone in her stomach.

'How soon?' she heard herself ask.

'If the progression continues at this rate? Another month, perhaps two. But Dimity—' His tone shifted, became more serious. 'You should be celebrating. This is wonderful news. Why do you look so troubled?'

She manufactured a smile. 'I'm not troubled. I'm overwhelmed. It's a lot to process.'

He seemed to accept this, but as she left his office, she felt the weight of her lie like a physical thing pressing against her chest.

Vivian noticed something was different as soon as she arrived back at the cottage.

'How did it go?' he asked, looking up from the manuscript spread across the kitchen table. She tried not to look at him.

'Well,' she said, hanging up her coat with hands that trembled slightly. 'Very well. Dr Hughes is pleased with my progress.'

'That's wonderful.' His voice was warm, genuine. 'I'm so happy for you.'

She wanted to tell him. Wanted to say: *I can see you. I can see the grey-green of your eyes, the way your hair falls across your forehead, the scar at your temple. I can see the way you look at me when you think I'm not aware of it.*

Instead, she said, 'Shall we get back to work? I think we're close to finishing Chapter Twenty-Three.'

The book was nearly complete. Another week, perhaps two, and they would be done. Dimity tried not to think about what would happen after that—when Vivian would pack his things and return to London, when the cottage would be hers alone again, when the manuscript would go off to the printers and she would have no reason to spend every day with him.

She tried not to think about it, but it was there in every shared meal, every reading, every moment of being together. The end was coming, inevitable as winter. Her life would go back to what it always had been. Dimity, not good enough to be a part of anything else than her own company and the world in her head.

The cottage, for its part, seemed determined to make the most of the time they had left. More mistletoe appeared daily. The fire burned warmer, brighter. The Christmas tree in the front room—which neither of them mentioned anymore, having silently agreed to accept it as one of Aunt Bea's inexplicable gifts—began to acquire ornaments that neither of them remembered placing.

'Did you put the silver bird on the tree?' Vivian asked one morning.

Dimity, who could now see the delicate ornament catching the light, shook her head. 'No. Did you?'

'No.'

They looked at each other, then at the tree.

'Aunt Bea,' they said together, and let it go.

##

Lila called on a Wednesday, her voice bubbling with barely contained excitement.

'I'm coming to visit. Tomorrow. Don't argue—I need to see you, I have news, and frankly, darling, I'm dying to meet this editor of yours properly. Not just a phone call, but in person.'

Dimity's heart stuttered. 'Lila, I don't think—'

'Tomorrow. Two o'clock. I'll bring lunch. See you then!' The line went dead before Dimity could protest further.

She stood holding the phone, panic rising in

her chest.

'Everything all right?' Vivian asked from across the room.

'Lila's coming tomorrow. To visit.'

'That's nice. You must miss her.'

She did miss Lila. But having her here, in the cottage, would make everything more real—more complicated. Lila would see things. Lila always saw things. She knew Dimity very well.

'Yes,' she said faintly. 'Yes, it will be lovely.'

•

Lila arrived at precisely two o'clock the next day, sweeping into the cottage like her usual determined whirlwind self. She held Dimity close and then turned her attention to Vivian with open curiosity.

'So, you're the famous award-winning Vivian Edwards,' she said, extending her hand. 'I've heard so much about you.'

'All good, I hope,' he replied, shaking her hand with a smile that Dimity could now see— warm, slightly bemused, genuinely kind. She couldn't stop looking at him.

'Most of it,' Lila said, her eyes twinkling. She'd brought lunch from a deli in Chipping

Norton—sandwiches, soup, fresh bread—and insisted they all eat together before any serious conversation could occur.

The meal was pleasant, filled with easy conversation and Lila's usual sharp wit. Dimity watched her two worlds collide—her dearest friend and the man she'd come to... what? Care for? Need? Love?

The thought made her chest tighten.

After lunch, Vivian excused himself to make some phone calls, giving the two women time together. The moment he was out of earshot, Lila turned to Dimity with an expression that was equal parts knowing and concerned.

'All right,' she said, 'talk to me. What's going on?'

'What do you mean?'

'Dimity. I know you. Something's different. You're... I don't know. Wound up. Anxious. And the way you look at him—' She paused. 'Or rather, the way you don't look at him, as if you're afraid of what you might see.'

Dimity's hands trembled. She set down her teacup carefully.

'I have feelings for him,' she said quietly. The admission, spoken aloud for the first time, felt like both a relief and a betrayal. 'I have feelings for Vivian, and I don't know what to do about it.'

Lila's face softened. 'Oh, darling. That's not exactly a surprise. Anyone with eyes could see the way you two are.' She reached out, taking Dimity's hand. 'But that's not all, is it? There's something else.'

Dimity closed her eyes. 'My vision is almost back. Sixty percent restored. Dr Hughes thinks it will be nearly complete within a month or two.'

'Dimity!' Lila's voice rang with joy. 'That's incredible! That's wonderful! Why didn't you tell me immediately? Why—' She stopped, understanding dawning. 'You haven't told Vivian either.'

'No.'

'Why not?'

'Because...' Dimity's voice broke. 'Because when my vision is fully restored, I won't need him anymore. There will be no reason for him to stay. We'll finish the book, and he'll go back to London, and I'll be alone again. At least now, I have an excuse. At least now, he has a reason to be here.'

'Oh, Dimity.' Lila squeezed her hand tightly.

'You can't build a relationship on dependency. If he has feelings for you—and I suspect he does, the way he looks at you when he thinks you're not aware—then your vision returning shouldn't change that.'

'But what if it does? What if I'm just a project to him? A manuscript to edit, a blind woman to help?'

'Is that really what you think of him?'

Dimity was silent.

'Listen to me,' Lila said firmly. 'You need to tell him. Both about your feelings and about your vision. Secrets like this have a way of festering. They rot relationships from the inside out.'

'I will,' Dimity whispered. 'I will. Just... not yet. Please.'

Lila sighed but nodded. 'All right. But soon, Dimity. Promise me.'

'I promise.'

'Now,' Lila said, her tone brightening deliberately, 'I have news that should cheer you up considerably. First: the Netflix contract is signed. They've officially optioned the series rights for a very handsome sum. Your solicitor has the details, but Dimity—you're going to be more than comfortable.'

Dimity felt tears prick her eyes. 'Lila, that's... I don't even know what to say.'

'Don't say anything yet, because I'm not done. Second piece of news: You're no longer with Moongate Publishing.'

'What?'

'Your contract is done,' Lila repeated, her voice firm and satisfied. 'You've gone back to being an independent publisher. But we can now hire someone to do all the back work: the formatting, the uploading, the advertising. All you have to do is write the stories.'

Joy flooded through Dimity; she had always known that Lila was the right choice to handle her career.

'I want to work with authors I believe in, authors I care about. I want to build something meaningful, not just profitable. And this Netflix deal? It's given us the capital to do exactly that.'

Dimity was overwhelmed, her emotions a tangled knot of joy and fear and gratitude. 'I don't know what to say.'

'Say you'll stay with me. Say you'll let me represent your next book, and the one after that.'

'Of course. Lila, you have me for life.'

They embraced, and Dimity's tears finally

spilled over.

Lila stayed for another hour, chatting about plans and timelines and all the exciting times ahead. Casting, filming, book tours, the schedule seemed endless. When Vivian joined them, they discussed the final chapters of the manuscript, the production schedule, and the marketing strategy. He was professional, insightful, and asked all the right questions.

But Dimity could see—truly see—the way his eyes kept drifting to her. The concern in his expression. The gentleness in every gesture.

When Lila finally left, pressing a kiss to Dimity's cheek and whispering, 'Tell him soon,' Dimity felt paralysed by indecision.

She didn't know what to do. The words she needed to say—*I can see you, I have feelings for you, I've been lying to you*—felt impossible to arrange in any order that wouldn't destroy everything. How did you confess something like this? Where did you even begin?

She couldn't trust herself to say the right things. Every possible conversation she imagined ended badly—with hurt in his voice, with professional distance replacing the warmth they'd built, with him packing his things and leaving her alone in this cottage that suddenly felt too big and too small all at once.

But she knew she had to be honest. Lila was right. Secrets festered. And Vivian deserved better than her cowardice, better than her convenient omissions, better than a woman who couldn't find the courage to tell him the truth.

She just didn't know how.

That night, she couldn't face dinner with Vivian. She made excuses about a headache, retreated to her room, and closed the door.

Then she sat on the edge of her bed and let herself fall apart.

She could see. She could see the room around her—Aunt Bea's wallpaper, the window overlooking the garden, the books on the nightstand. She could see the tears on her own hands when she lifted them to her face.

And she was keeping it all secret, lying by omission to the person who mattered most to her.

Lila was right. Secrets festered. They rotted things from the inside.

But telling the truth meant facing the possibility of loss—of Vivian leaving, of her fragile happiness crumbling, of being alone again in this cottage that had given her back so much.

She didn't know which frightened her more: the lie she was living, or the truth she was too afraid to speak.

Outside her window, snow began to fall— soft, silent, covering the garden in white. In the room below, she could hear Vivian moving quietly, banking the fire, tidying the kitchen.

Taking care of her, as he had for weeks now.

Taking care of her, while she lied to his face.

Dimity buried her face in her hands and wept.

Chapter Sixteen

The days passed quickly as they worked, talked and shared comfortable silences around the fire each evening. With each morning, Dimity's vision sharpened—shadows becoming shapes, shapes finding edges, colours returning her world like pale watercolours. She could see the firelight dancing on the walls now, the familiar spines of Bea's books, the way Vivian's hands moved when he gestured while reading. But she told no one, afraid that speaking it aloud might break the spell—or worse, give Vivian a reason to leave.

Dimity stood at the kitchen window, mug in hand, watching the faint movement of branches against the brightening sky. She could see almost everything now—the outline of the trees, the soft rise of the hills beyond the garden wall. Every glimpse of light was a miracle. And yet it filled her with unease.

She had waited too long to tell Vivian. She had ruined any chance of a happy ending. How would she have written it?

She shook her head. She had written it. Elara had been honest, and she had her happy ending. Finally, in book five of the series.

Would it take her that long to find happiness in her own life?

From the sitting room came the soft murmur of Vivian's voice, low and measured as he read through the final proof pages. The sound steadied her, even as her heart clenched at the knowledge that soon he'd be gone.

Mrs Willoughby had brought mince pies the day before and a cheerful invitation to the village dinner at the church hall. Dimity had accepted politely, knowing she wouldn't go. The idea of company, of smiling through well-meaning conversation while her chest ached with confusion, was unbearable.

'You're very quiet this morning,' Vivian said from the doorway. His tone was gentle, careful.

'Just tired,' she replied, setting her mug down.

'It's Christmas, Dimity. Even writers are allowed to rest on Christmas.'

She turned towards him, heart thudding at how clearly she could see him now—the tousled hair, the open collar of his shirt, the faint shadow along his jaw. He looked… ordinary, but in a way that made her breath catch. Kind eyes, capable hands, a steadiness she had come to lean on.

'I'm resting,' she said softly.

He smiled, but it didn't quite reach his eyes. 'Mrs Willoughby insists I join them for lunch. You should come.'

'I think I'll stay here,' she said quickly. 'The crowds, the noise… it'll be easier if I don't.'

Vivian nodded once, understanding more than she wanted him to. 'Then I'll bring you back something. Save you a mince pie.'

'Thank you.'

##

When he left, the silence folded in around her like a heavy shawl. She sat in Aunt Bea's chair, phone on the side table, thumb hovering over the call button. It was Christmas—she couldn't avoid it forever.

Her mother answered on the second ring, brisk as ever. 'Dimity! Finally! I was beginning to think you'd forgotten your family entirely.'

'Happy Christmas, Mum.'

There was a pause — long enough for Dimity to picture the familiar kitchen at the farm worlds away, at the farm at Yungaburra—her mother at the bench, her father reading the paper in the next room.

'So, how are you? You sound better,' her mother said. 'Is the doctor happy with your recovery?'

Dimity swallowed. 'I'm improving every day.' Not a lie, she told herself. Just not the whole truth.

'Good. Then perhaps it's time you thought about coming home. You've been in England long enough, haven't you? There's a job going at the pharmacy again—'

'Mum,' she interrupted gently. 'I'm not coming home.'

'What? You've been gone too long. What on earth are you doing there?'

'I'm working. Writing.'

A soft scoff down the line. 'Still that nonsense? You could be earning a proper living here.'

The old ache rose, familiar and sharp. 'Mum, I'm twenty-four. This is my life. I need to find out who I am before I come back.

If I ever go back.

The silence that followed was the one she

knew—tight, disapproving, full of things unsaid. She could almost see Mum's lips pressed thin, her fingers drumming the bench in frustration.

Finally, her father's voice came faintly in the background. 'Give the girl a chance, love. It's Christmas.'

Her mother sighed. 'Fine. But promise you'll at least call more often.'

'I will. Merry Christmas, Mum. Love to Dad, too.'

She ended the call gently, but her hands were trembling. Relief mingled with guilt, but for the first time, she didn't let it crush her.

##

She scrolled to another number. 'Lila,' she said when her friend answered, her voice warming.

'Dimity! Merry Christmas, love. Marcus and I were just talking about you.'

Dimity smiled. 'You're not working?'

'Not today. Even literary agents get a holiday. How's my favourite writer?'

'Better,' she admitted. 'The manuscript's finished. We're on the final proof.'

Lila squealed so loudly that Dimity had to hold the phone away. 'Finished? That's wonderful! And how's your gorgeous editor?'

'Professional. Brilliant. Infuriatingly calm.'

'In other words, you like him,' Lila teased. 'Or more?'

Dimity hesitated. 'Maybe.'

'We're coming to the Cotswolds for New Year's,' Lila said suddenly. 'Marcus wants to see this magical cottage I've told him about. New Year's Eve, if that suits?'

Dimity felt her heart lift. 'It would be perfect.'

'Good. You can tell me everything when we arrive.'

When the call ended, she felt a little better. Lila would cheer her up; they would be finished and Vivian would be gone this week.

But her relief didn't last. As she sat staring into the fire, her thoughts spiralled — through every moment she'd spent with Vivian, every silence that had said more than words. She realised, with a hollow ache, that she was in love with him.

She thought of his patience, the way he'd listened without judgment. Of how he'd made her world brighter when hers had been dark.

And now, when she'd finally found her

footing again—when her sight was returning, when she could have shared everything—he would be gone.

Her throat tightened. 'You can't keep running from what you feel,' she whispered into the empty room. 'You promised Bea you'd live.'

The air shifted. The faint scent of vanilla and almond—Aunt Bea's Christmas biscuits—drifted through the air.

'All right,' she murmured. 'I understand. I get it. I know what I have to do.'

She dressed quickly, wrapping herself in her coat and scarf, and stepped out into the snow.

Chapter Seventeen

The world outside shimmered with light. Snowflakes caught the glow of streetlamps, and the air was so still that Dimity could hear her own heartbeat. She walked to Mrs Willoughby's cottage, hoping she'd find Vivian there.

Mrs Willoughby opened the door, her cheeks pink, her arms dusted with flour.

'Well, look who's out and about!' she exclaimed. 'Merry Christmas, my dear!'

'Merry Christmas. I was hoping to catch Mr Edwards before he went to the church?'

'He's already there,' Mrs Willoughby said. Then she paused, eyes narrowing as she took in Dimity's face. 'Wait… you can see me.'

Dimity froze, startled. 'I—yes. I can.'

'Oh, my love!' Mrs Willoughby clasped her hands, eyes bright with tears. 'It's back, isn't it? Your sight!'

Dimity nodded, emotion breaking her composure. 'A little at first, then more each day. I was too afraid to tell anyone — not until I told him.'

'Then don't stand here telling me!' the older woman said, laughing through tears. 'Go to him, before that snow buries the world.'

Dimity smiled, her vision blurring for a new reason. 'Thank you. I'll wait at Pippin's Nook.'

As she turned to leave, Mrs Willoughby pressed a mittened hand to her chest, overcome with delight.

'Oh, this will make his Christmas!' she said, and before Dimity was halfway down the path, she'd pulled her shawl tighter and was already bustling the other way—towards the church.

***

Vivian sat alone in a pew near the back, the distant sound of carols echoing through the stone nave. The warmth from the nearby heater did little to reach the chill inside him.

He'd spent half the morning trying not to think of Dimity—of her laughter, her courage, the way she'd tilted her head when she was listening. He had fallen for her completely. And that terrified him.

Dimity deserved a future—one unburdened by his failures. What kind of man fell in love with a woman he was paid to help? What kind of writer couldn't even finish his own story?

He leaned forward, pressing a hand to his forehead. 'You're an idiot,' he muttered under his breath. 'You should have kept your distance.'

'Mr Edwards!'

He turned. Mrs Willoughby stood at the back of the church, breathless, cheeks flushed. 'She can see! Our Dimity can see again!'

Vivian rose slowly. 'She... what?'

'Her sight's come back. She's on her way home to tell you!'

For a moment, joy flared—bright, fierce— and then died almost instantly.

She could see.

And now she would see him: not the steady voice that guided her through darkness, but the man who had hidden behind professionalism and borrowed confidence.

'That's wonderful news,' he said quietly. 'Truly.'

Mrs Willoughby looked puzzled. 'Aren't you coming?'

But he only shook his head, the decision forming before he could stop it.

'I think it's best if I give her space,' he said.

He left the church, walking quickly through the snow towards his car.

When Dimity returned to Pippin's Nook, the cottage was warm, the fire glowing softly. She set down her gloves, her heart full and light. She would tell him everything—about her sight, her fear, and the truth she'd been too afraid to speak.

She heard the front door open and turned with a smile.

'Vivian! I—'

But he was already crossing the room, coat in hand, his expression shuttered.

'Dimity,' he said quietly. 'I came to say goodbye. The agency called. They've decided to move up my reassignment. I have to leave this afternoon.'

His words struck her square in the chest, and for a moment, she couldn't breathe. 'But… it's Christmas Day—'

'I'm sorry.' His tone was soft but distant, every word deliberate. 'It's better this way. You'll be fine—better than fine. You're remarkable.'

He began to gather his things, his movements brisk, avoiding her gaze.

'Vivian, wait. Please—'

But he was already at the door. He hesitated, just once, as though he might turn back. Then he said simply, 'Merry Christmas, Dimity,' and was gone.

She ran to the window, breath fogging the glass. His figure blurred in the falling snow before he got into his car, leaving only the hollow echo of tyres on frost as it vanished down the lane.

The cottage settled around her in aching stillness.

The fire crackled softly. The candles on the mantel burned low.

And somewhere, faint but certain, came the scent of vanilla and almond — Bea's quiet reminder that nothing truly ended here.

Chapter Eighteen

Morning crept softly into Pippin's Nook, brushing the frost-framed windows with pale gold. Dimity stirred, eyes opening to a wash of light that made her breath catch. For the first time in months, the world was whole again.

She sat up slowly, the blanket sliding into her lap, the simple act of seeing overwhelming in its quiet enormity. Shadows, shapes, the faint blue gleam of the morning sky through the glass — everything was there, steady and vivid.

Her vision had returned. Completely.

And he was gone.

The memory of the door closing the night before lingered—that soft, final click, and the hollow stillness that followed. Vivian's voice, low and apologetic. *It's better this way. You'll be fine — better than fine.*

She pressed a hand to her chest, her heartbeat heavy against her palm.

You're wrong, she thought. *Nothing feels fine.*

The cottage was too quiet. Even the fire had

burned low in the grate, its faint orange coals dull and tired. She rose, made tea on autopilot, and stood at the sink, watching the first light creep across the garden wall. Every detail sharpened—the faint cracks in the window frame, the long reach of ivy across the gate, the glint of frost on the old birdbath.

All of it more beautiful than she remembered. All of it hollow without Vivian.

She found her phone on the table and dialled his number. Once. Twice. Three times. Each time, it rang into silence, then clicked to voicemail. She didn't leave a message. What could she say?

Come back. I can see now. I need you.

The words felt too large, too late.

By midday, she was pacing the sitting room, unable to settle. Her eyes caught on the desk—the pages of her manuscript, neatly stacked, his pencilled notes in the margins. She traced a line of his handwriting.

It was all she had left of him.

When she could bear the cottage no longer, she wrapped herself in her coat and stepped outside. The cold was knife-sharp, cutting through her clothes, but she welcomed it. It made her feel real. The lane wound empty towards the village, the snow from Christmas Day flattened into grey slush.

Mrs Willoughby's curtains twitched as she passed. Moments later, the door opened.

'Dimity! Oh, my dear—come in, you'll freeze out there.'

'No, thank you,' Dimity said gently. 'I was just walking.'

The older woman frowned. 'You look pale. Where's that nice Mr Edwards? Off visiting family, is he?'

Dimity forced a smile. 'He's gone back to Oxford. His work here's finished.'

Mrs Willoughby's hand flew to her chest. 'Gone? But… he was such a help to you. And so fond of you, too, I could tell.'

Dimity's throat tightened. 'He was kind. That's all.'

'Kind men don't look at women the way he looked at you,' Mrs Willoughby said shrewdly. Then her expression softened. 'You poor love. You'll find your feet. The cottage has a way of holding on to those who need it most.'

Dimity nodded, unable to trust her voice, and continued down the lane.

##

The week that followed unfolded in fragments, like pages turned too slowly.

She cleaned, though nothing needed cleaning. Rearranged the books on Bea's shelves, only to move them back again. The cottage hummed around her, protesting—the faint creak of beams, the whisper of the wind at the chimney —its presence gentle but insistent, as if waiting for her to listen.

Each morning, she rose before dawn, making tea and sitting by the window to watch the first blush of light spill across the orchard. Each night she wrote—not chapters, not stories, just thoughts, questions, small confessions she'd never dared speak aloud.

You made me believe I could see again, long before I actually could. You left before I could tell you that you healed more than my eyes.

Her phone remained silent. She checked it anyway.

Mrs Willoughby continued her daily visits, sometimes bringing soup, sometimes gossip. She spoke of the village choir, the vicar's new Labrador, and the Christmas fair. Always, at the end, she would sigh and say, 'It's not right, a young woman alone at Christmas.'

Dimity would smile faintly, thank her, and close the door, her chest aching with the same thought.

##

By the end of the week, the snow had begun to thaw. Dimity walked into the village on Saturday, the ground slick beneath her boots. The high street was busy with families and the soft rumble of laughter spilling from the bakery.

She stopped by the grocer's stall, bought apples, candles, and a small notebook with a marbled blue cover. The man behind the counter grinned.

'You're the writer, aren't you? Mrs Willoughby mentioned you.'

Dimity blinked. 'I suppose I am.'

'Well, welcome to Lower Thistlewick, then. Always room for another storyteller here.'

His words—kind, ordinary—cheered her. She walked home slowly, the notebook tucked under her arm.

I'll write, she thought. Even if it's just for me. I've always been alone; I can be again.

But that night, sitting by the fire, she felt the faintest shift in the air—a warmth rising from the old floorboards, the quiet crackle of something around her. The scent of almonds and sugar drifted briefly through the room, gone as quickly as it came.

'You don't agree with my choice, do you, Bea?' she whispered.

A soft creak came from the beams above, the kind that sounded suspiciously like laughter.

Dimity smiled sadly. 'You always were a meddler.'

##

New Year's Eve arrived with a sky the colour of pewter and a silence so deep it felt absolute. Dimity spent the morning tidying—not for guests, but because movement kept her from breaking. She made soup, lit candles, arranged holly in the jug on the mantel. The small rituals steadied her hands but not her heart. It made her think of the mistletoe. All that mistletoe that had appeared at Christmas, and they had never once kissed.

The sound of tyres crunching on the lane startled her. She went to the window. A dark car, familiar and foreign, rolled to a stop.

Lila stepped out first, bundled in a red scarf, her face bright despite the cold. Marcus followed, carrying a bottle of champagne.

Dimity opened the door before they could knock.

'You look beautiful,' Lila said immediately, pulling her into a hug. 'And you can see! Oh, thank heaven for that.'

'Yes,' Dimity whispered. 'I can.'

'Then why do you look as though you've lost everything?'

Dimity laughed softly, the sound thin and weary. 'Because I might have.'

Lila's eyes softened. 'He hasn't been in touch?'

'No. Not a word.'

Marcus appeared behind her, setting the champagne on the hall table. 'I'll start a fire,' he said quietly, sensing their need to talk and slipping away.

Lila turned back to Dimity. 'You know, when he rang to tell me he'd left, his voice cracked halfway through. He said you were the bravest person he'd ever met.'

Dimity frowned. 'He called you?'

'He did. To make sure I'd check in on you.'

That simple truth broke something inside her. She turned away, blinking hard. 'Then why didn't he call me?'

'Because men are idiots,' Lila said simply. 'Especially the ones who fall in love and think they don't deserve it.'

Dimity shook her head. 'He left because he saw me clearly and realised there was nothing left to keep him here.'

'No, darling,' Lila said gently. 'He left because he thought you didn't need him anymore. Because you never told him you did.'

Dimity's breath hitched.

'He's not far,' Lila continued. 'Oxford didn't call him back after all. He's renting a cottage near Burford. Twenty minutes away.'

Dimity stared at her, heart pounding. 'How do you know?'

'I have my ways,' Lila said with a small smile. 'Now, are you going to sit here all night feeling sorry for yourself, or are we going to fix this before the year ends?'

'I can't just turn up—'

'Yes, you can. You love him. And unless you want to start next year regretting what you didn't say, you'd better get your coat.'

Chapter Nineteen

The week after Christmas blurred into sameness—days marked not by hours but by the slow, aching stillness that settled over Vivian like a fog that wouldn't lift.

Foolishly, he'd thought leaving Pippin's Nook would ease the unhappiness that filled him. Instead, it had followed him here—into this narrow, draughty place with its low beams and single window that looked onto a field rimmed with bare trees.

He missed the hum of the cottage.

He missed *her*.

The small sitting room bore the evidence of his restlessness: pages of half-started paragraphs scattered across the table, pencil shavings curling like woodchips, an untouched mug of tea growing cold beside the lamp. He'd tried to write—not edit, not refine someone else's work, but truly write—and found nothing in him. The words he'd once believed in had abandoned him, just as he'd abandoned the one person who had made them feel possible again.

The fire crackled weakly in the grate, throwing uneven light across the walls. The room smelled faintly of ash and damp wool. He pulled the blanket tighter around his shoulders and stared at the notebook in his lap. A single line filled the top of the page:

She had learned to see long before her sight returned.

He let out a breath that trembled more than he'd intended.

Every morning since he'd left, he'd told himself it was the right thing. Dimity needed space to heal, to rediscover her independence without him leaning too close, without his presence reminding her of what she'd lost. He had been hired to help, not to fall in love with her voice, her courage, her words, the way she could laugh at herself even through fear.

Yet the silence of this cottage pressed on him like a held breath.

He'd begun hearing Dimity in the smallest things—the soft clink of a spoon against a mug, the whisper of paper turning, the way the kettle began to hum before it boiled. In Pippin's Nook, those sounds had been life; here, they were ghosts.

Vivian leaned back in the chair, eyes tracing the firelight. The last time he'd seen her, she'd been standing in the doorway, her hand resting lightly on the frame. He hadn't even been able to look at her properly. The words he'd rehearsed— thank you, goodbye—had stuck somewhere behind his ribcage.

He'd told himself it was mercy. That leaving before she saw the truth—before she looked at him with pity instead of trust—was the kinder choice.

Because what would she see, really? A man past thirty-five with a face marked by old scars, a failed novelist who'd built a career polishing other people's stories. Not the hero she wrote about, nor the man she deserved. So, he was the editor of the year? That meant nothing. Other people had written those words.

The wind rattled the panes, and he rose, crossing to the window. Beyond the glass, the field shimmered with frost, pale under the last light of the year. A hare darted across the edge of the hedgerow, its shape swift and fleeting.

He rested his forehead against the cold glass.

You fool, he thought. You should have stayed.

Later, he sat at his desk, pen poised over the empty page, the ink refusing to flow. The fire had burned to embers, its glow faint and sullen. He rubbed his eyes, fatigue settling into his bones. Each member of his family had called, and he had ignored every call and let them all go to voicemail. He knew his parents; if he didn't call back in a day or so, they would track him down and turn up on the doorstep of this depressing cottage. This dead, lifeless cottage with no magic.

Because he finally admitted to himself that yes, Pippin's Nook held magic.

Dimity brought magic to him, too.

He thought of her voice when she dictated—tentative at first, then growing stronger, the rhythm of her sentences as familiar now as his own heartbeat. He thought of her laughter, low and warm when she caught him mispronouncing one of her invented fae words.

He thought of the way the cottage had seemed to breathe when she was near—how the air itself was full of life.

Since he'd left, even the weather had turned sullen. No snow at all in Burford, just rain that smeared the horizon into dull grey streaks and left sludge on the ground.

He picked up the notebook again and stared at the single line. Then, slowly, he crossed it out.

***

The drive passed in silence. The sky had deepened to indigo, the edges of the landscape blurred by falling snow. Lila's headlights carved a narrow path through the white, the car's heater humming softly.

Dimity sat rigid in the passenger seat, her hands clasped in her lap. The closer they came to Burford, the louder her heart seemed to beat.

'You can do this,' Lila said gently.

'I can,' Dimity whispered. 'The cottage won't let me rest until I do.'

Lila smiled faintly. 'Then I'll wait in the car. Go knock on his door, Dim.'

The cottage was small, a single light burning in the front room. Smoke curled from the chimney, thin and wavering.

Dimity climbed the stone steps, her boots crunching in the snow. She paused at the door, breath misting in the air. Behind her, the wind hushed, and in the distance a church bell began to chime midnight — twelve slow, resonant notes that seemed to echo across the valley.

She closed her eyes.

'Please,' she whispered into the night—to Bea, to the cottage that had healed her, to whatever magic listened. 'Please let him open the door.'

The final chime faded. She raised her hand and knocked.

The sound hung in the stillness, soft but certain.

Behind her, the snow fell heavier, the world holding its breath.

And in that perfect, suspended moment — before footsteps stirred on the other side of the door — the magic of Pippin's Nook reached across the fields, its gentle enchantment curling through the air like a promise.

***

By late afternoon, the light had faded. Vivian made soup and didn't eat it. Poured whisky and didn't drink it.

Somewhere down the lane, a clock struck nine.

He thought of going to bed, but couldn't bear the thought of lying in darkness with only his own regret for company. So, he stayed by the fire instead, watching the flames sink lower.

The silence thickened until it seemed to fill him.

He told himself it was the wind, the shifting of old timbers. But beneath that was something else—a pulse of warmth, faint but distinct.

For a heartbeat, the room smelled faintly of almonds and sugar.

He frowned, straightening in his chair. The scent was impossible—and unmistakable. Bea's biscuits. Dimity had told him that story one evening, her voice soft with affection as she spoke of her aunt and the cottage's peculiar magic.

A warmth stirred low in his chest, equal parts longing and disbelief.

'Don't be ridiculous,' he muttered aloud. 'It's memory. Nothing more.'

And then—three soft knocks at the door.

He froze.

Another knock, firmer this time.

Vivian's heart jolted painfully. He rose too quickly, the chair legs scraping the floor. For a moment, he stood motionless, staring at the door, afraid to hope.

Outside, the wind had dropped. The world was utterly still.

He crossed the room slowly, his pulse roaring in his ears. His hand hovered over the latch.

'Dimity?' he whispered.

The third knock came, quiet but certain, as if in answer.

He drew a breath, his hand shaking as he turned the handle.

Chapter Twenty

For a heartbeat, neither of them moved. The cold night pressed in behind her, the warmth of his cottage at her back, and somewhere between the two stood everything unsaid.

Vivian's hand still gripped the door. The lamplight spilled out behind him, catching the faint lines of fatigue on his face—the week of silence carved there. His eyes, the grey of winter, searched hers as if afraid she might disappear in the next gust of wind.

'Dimity,' he breathed at last, disbelief breaking softly in his voice.

'You left,' she said, and her voice cracked. 'You left without letting me tell you.'

The words trembled between them. Then he stepped aside, his composure faltering. 'You'd better come in. It's freezing.'

The room was smaller than she'd imagined, its low beams dark with age. A single chair beside the hearth, a table littered with paper and half-written notes, a kettle steaming faintly on the hob. The smell of ink and smoke and loneliness pervaded the depressing space.

Vivian shut the door and stood a little apart, shoulders stiff, as though he didn't quite know what to do with himself. 'I didn't think—' He stopped, the sentence fraying. 'I thought you'd—'

'That I'd what?' she asked quietly.

He met her gaze, and the truth she saw there was raw. 'That you'd already begun to move past me. That you didn't need me once your sight returned.'

Dimity swallowed hard. 'You assumed I could see again?'

'I knew.' He nodded once. 'Mrs Willoughby found me at the church on Christmas Day. She could hardly contain herself—she was so happy for you. She told me—she was so delighted she could hardly get the words out. And I—' He broke off, his mouth tightening. 'I thought it was the sign I'd been waiting for. That the cottage had finished what I never could.'

The silence that followed was sharp as glass. Dimity drew a breath that felt too large for her lungs. 'You think my sight was all that mattered?'

'It mattered to me,' he said simply. 'Because

you deserved your world back. Not the narrow one I'd built around you.'

'You fool,' she whispered.

His head jerked up, startled, but there was no anger in her face—only hurt, and something warmer beneath it. She stepped closer, her hands trembling, though her voice stayed calm. 'You talk about the world as if it's light and distance. But you were the first thing I saw clearly—long before my eyes worked again. And you left me in the darkness. After I could see again.'

He took a half-step forward, then stopped. 'I didn't want you to see what I am.'

'What you are,' she said, 'is the only man who made me believe my stories weren't foolish dreams.'

The air between them quivered with longing. A log fell into the grate, a small reminder that time was still moving even if neither of them could.

Dimity exhaled shakily and reached for her phone, fingers clumsy on the screen. 'I need to tell Lila I'm safe before she sends out a search party.'

Vivian blinked, still dazed. 'Lila's here?'

'In the car. Down the lane. She brought me.'

Dimity gave him a glance that dared him to argue. 'I told her I wasn't leaving until you listened to me.'

He made a rough sound that might have been a laugh. 'That sounds like you.'

'It sounds like the new me,' she corrected. Then she lifted the phone. 'Lila? Yes, I found him. No, I'm not leaving yet. You go back to the cottage and Marcus. We'll come later. Yes, together.' Her smile softened. 'Thank you, my friend.'

When she ended the call, the quiet returned, but it had changed. Something in the room eased, as if it had been holding its breath too.

'You shouldn't have come in this weather,' Vivian said at last, his tone gentle but strained. 'The roads are dreadful.'

'I've lived through worse than slippery lanes,' she replied. 'I couldn't start a new year with a lie between us.'

He looked down at the notebook on the table; pages scattered like confessions. 'There were no words left to send,' he murmured. 'I tried to write. Every line came out hollow.'

'Then perhaps you needed a different kind of sentence,' she said softly.

Her words made him look up. For the first time, she saw past the facade—the tiredness, the uncertainty, and something deeper—shame, perhaps, that he'd dared to care.

He gestured to the fire. 'Sit. Please.'

Dimity obeyed, perched on the edge of the chair while he crouched to stir the coals. Sparks flared, catching a faint scar that ran from his jaw to his temple, silvered in the lamplight.

'I used to think scars meant failure,' he said quietly, catching her gaze on his face. 'That I'd failed to become what I meant to. Writer, friend, man. My scar represents my failings. You made me want to try again, and I hated myself for it.'

'You think I care about a scar?' she whispered.

'I think you deserve someone whole.'

'Then you don't know me at all,' Dimity said. 'I was never whole until I broke.'

The honesty in her voice undid him. He rose slowly, as if any sudden motion might shatter the fragile link they'd built. When he reached her, he hesitated only a breath before taking her hands.

Her fingers were cold from the drive; his were trembling. For a long moment, neither spoke.

Then, he said softly, 'I loved every word you dictated. Not the stories themselves—the courage in them. Every line was you learning to live again, and I had the privilege of hearing it first.'

Tears blurred her vision. 'Then why did you leave before you let me say thank you?'

'Because I wanted you to see the world, not me.'

She smiled through the ache. 'You are the world, Vivian. Or at least the part that finally made sense. My world.'

He bent his head then, uncertain until the moment their foreheads touched. The contact was small, almost accidental, but the tremor that went through her felt infinite. His breath mingled with hers, warm against the hush of the room.

'Dimity,' he whispered. 'If you knew how I've missed you—'

'I know,' she said, her voice steady now. 'Because I've missed me, too. The person I was when you were there.'

He laughed softly, the sound breaking on a sigh. 'You always win the argument.'

'Then let me win this one as well. Come home.'

'Home?'

'To Pippin's Nook. Tonight. We can see the new year in properly—by starting over.'

He hesitated. 'Do you think the house will forgive me?'

'It's just a house,' she said, smiling. 'But yes. It will.'

He stepped closer, brushed a curl from her cheek. 'Thank you for finding me.'

'You weren't lost,' she whispered. 'Just waiting for the story to catch up.'

And then, finally, he kissed her—slowly, and with love, as if each breath were a promise not to vanish again.

They didn't speak for a long time after that. The fire popped; somewhere outside, a church bell chimed.

Vivian drew her into his arms, resting his chin on her hair. 'You know,' he said softly, 'I still don't believe in magic.'

'That's all right,' she murmured against his shoulder. 'It believes in you.'

He smiled, closing his eyes, and for the first time in years, the ache inside him stilled. The cottage held them quietly, no magic—just the honesty of homecoming.

When he finally pulled back, Dimity reached for her phone again.

'Lila?' she said when the line connected. 'Yes. We're coming home.'

She ended the call and set the phone on the table.

'What did she say?' he asked.

'That the cottage always knows.'

He laughed softly, taking her hand again. 'Then perhaps it knew we'd find our way, even when we didn't.'

'Perhaps,' she said. 'But from here on, let's make our own kind of magic.'

The flames burned lower, casting long shadows across the room. Outside, the snow fell steadily, whitening the world anew.

Vivian reached for the notebook he'd carried with him from his cottage, its first line still crossed out. He opened it to a fresh page, looked at Dimity, and wrote:

She had learned to see long before her sight returned—but now she chose what to see.

He laid the pen down and smiled. 'New beginnings,' he said quietly.

Dimity rested her head on his shoulder. 'Yes,' she murmured. 'And this time, together.'

Chapter Twenty-One

They left an hour later. Vivian locked the door behind them, his breath rising in pale clouds. The snow had begun again—fine, glittering flakes that swirled in the street lamplight as he drove down the lane to where Lila's tyre tracks had half-vanished under the drift.

The drive was quiet, their hands occasionally brushing on the gearshift. When the lights of Lower Thistlewick appeared through the dark, Dimity felt something inside her ease. The village looked unchanged—wreaths still on the doors, candles glowing faintly in the windows— but she saw it now with new eyes.

They reached the turn for Pippin's Nook just before midnight. The lane was narrow, the hedges dusted white, the stone wall of the orchard glimmering faintly in the car's headlights. Vivian stopped the engine, and for a moment neither of them moved.

'You're sure?' he asked quietly.

Dimity nodded. 'I've never been surer of anything in my life, or my stories.'

They climbed out, crunching through the snow towards the gate. The cottage loomed ahead, golden light flickering in the windows. Mrs Willoughby must have lit the lamps, but it looked almost as if the house had been waiting for them.

Dimity smiled. 'See? It's forgiving us already.'

Vivian glanced at her, wonder flickering in his eyes. 'I'd forgotten how alive this place feels.'

'That's because it listens,' she said, her tone half-teasing, half-reverent.

'Ready?' he asked.

'Home,' she said simply.

They crunched up the path together. Vivian unlocked the door, and it opened easily, as if relieved. Warm air and the faintest ghosts of lavender and beeswax welcomed them. From the sitting room came a flurry of movement, the rustle of wool and laughter sliding into relief.

'Finally!' Lila burst through the archway, scarf askew, eyes bright. 'You ridiculous pair.'

Marcus appeared behind her with a tray

balanced in his hands. 'We held off the champagne with a degree of heroism I think deserves recognition.'

'You mean you drank the first bottle and saved the second,' Lila said.

'Semantics,' Marcus replied mildly. 'Welcome home.'

Dimity stepped into Lila's arms and let herself be held. 'You were right,' she whispered.

'I always am,' Lila said fondly. 'But I prefer hearing you say it.'

Dimity turned towards Vivian, but Lila had already swept him into a quick, bossy embrace. 'Don't hurt her,' she said into his shoulder.

'That was never the danger,' he answered. 'The danger was always me leaving.'

'Then don't.' Lila's eyes softened. 'Stay for the new year. See what happens when you both decide to be brave at the same time.'

Marcus set the tray on the table with a clink of glasses. 'There's a tradition where I'm from,' he said. 'At midnight, you open the back door to let the old year out and the front to let the new year in.'

'It's freezing,' Lila said. 'But poetic.'

'We can do poetic,' Dimity said, smiling.

As Dimity watched, Vivian's gaze moved over the room—the tree with its baubles, the armchair with Bea's guardian birds worn smooth at the arms. Something in his face loosened, as if a knot had given way. He took the log basket to the hearth, added two pieces with a careful hand, and the fire caught with an eager rush, flames shouldering into brightness.

Dimity felt the cottage breathe around them. Not a trick of air, not a draught, but the quiet sense of welcome that had been hers since childhood. Tonight, it felt bigger—encompassing not only her grief and courage, but the man who had walked beside her.

Lila nudged Dimity towards the kitchen. 'Come on. I made midnight snacks, and they're not going to plate themselves.'

On the counter sat a small army of offerings: sausage rolls still warm, a plate of mince pies dusted lightly with sugar, wedges of sharp cheddar, and a bowl of glossy black olives. As Dimity reached for a platter, a sweetness folded through the air: vanilla, butter, almond—the exact scent of Christmases past. She paused, breath catching.

'You smell it?' she asked, low.

Lila sniffed. 'Mince pies?'

'Something else,' Dimity said. She didn't name it. She didn't need to. The cottage, discreet as ever, let the aroma drift and soften, like a hand brushed along her hair in blessing.

They carried food to the sitting room. Marcus uncorked the champagne with a sigh rather than a pop. He poured generously. Bubbles rose like a tide.

'A preliminary toast,' he announced. 'To long stories, late courage, and cottages that smell better than they have any right to.'

'Hear, hear,' Lila said, raising her glass.

They ate, they talked, and the room gathered their voices like light. They laughed until their eyes shone.

Dimity listened, happiness filling her in a way she'd never known before. She caught Vivian watching her in the slant of lamplight—hesitant at first, then more openly, as if the act of looking was a right they'd both earned.

'Tell us your plan,' Lila said at last, as the mantel clock tripped towards midnight. 'You two. What now?'

Dimity glanced at Vivian. He nodded, an invitation.

'I'll finish the final proof tomorrow,' she said. 'We'll send it. And then—' she swallowed, the shape of the future fragile but gleaming '— I'll start the next book here. With slower mornings and less fear. With some company, if he would like to stay.'

Vivian set down his glass. 'I do want to stay. I'll still take assignments, but… I want to write again. And I can't seem to imagine doing that anywhere but here. With you.'

Lila's grin could have lit the room. 'Excellent.'

Marcus raised his glass. 'To staying, then.'

'To staying,' Dimity echoed, her voice not quite steady.

From somewhere in the walls came the faintest sound—like the soft exhale of someone pleased. The tree lights brightened almost imperceptibly for a second or two. A candle near Bea's photograph flared and faded.

Dimity felt tears prick and let them. The magic was not about being a spectacle or a trick. It was all about blessing. The kind you only heard when you'd finally gone quiet enough inside.

The clock on the mantel lifted its hands.

Marcus checked his watch. 'One minute.'

'Right,' Lila said briskly, standing. 'Back door, front door. Let's give the old year a dignified exit.'

They crossed the small kitchen. Vivian lifted the back latch; cold night breathed in, crisp with frost and a hint of apple bark. A scatter of old leaves scudded across the threshold as if grateful to be released. The orchard stood at attention across the brilliant snow.

At the same moment, Dimity opened the front door. The lane lay white and clean, the air pricked with a thousand silent stars. A breeze slid past her like silk, and beneath it, a sound like distant water running towards spring.

'Goodbye, year,' Lila said, half-mocking, half-sincere. 'You were… a game changer.'

'You were necessary,' Dimity whispered. 'Thank you.'

They closed both doors as the clock chimed twelve. The sound rolled warmly through the rooms, the fire answering with a proud crackle. Vivian turned to her, his hand finding hers the way breath finds lungs.

'Happy New Year, my love,' he said, his eyes holding hers.

'Happy New Year,' she returned, and did not let go.

They toasted again, foolishly and grandly. To sight. To sentences. To fae lords. To fantasy worlds. To Elara. To the kind of quiet that heals. To Great Aunt Bea and Arthur.

Marcus put on a scratchy record he'd found in a charity shop—an old waltz with a horn that wavered in and out of tune—and for three minutes they let themselves be ridiculous. Lila danced with Marcus for half the song and then, with a squeal, claimed Vivian for the other half, passing him back to Dimity with a flourish that made them cheer.

After, breathless and amused, they collapsed into chairs and cushions. The talk turned softer, the way it does after midnight when the new year is still pristine and the old one has forgiven you. Lila quizzed Vivian mercilessly about his unwritten novel; he answered without deflecting, something near to hope loosening his voice. Marcus mapped out a plan for a village bonfire in February, on the precise night winter loosens its grip, because he believed in such things. They made outrageous resolutions for the months ahead, then scaled them back to achievable goals.

At some point, Lila stood and stretched. 'We should leave you two to your… staying.'

'Subtle,' Marcus said.

'Efficient,' Lila corrected.

'You should stay,' Dimity insisted.

'The cottage we've booked is in the village. We could walk if it wasn't so cold.' Lila kissed Dimity's forehead, squeezed Vivian's shoulder, and gave the mantel a pleased nod, as if Bea herself sat there supervising the festivities. 'Text me in the morning if you need anything. Or at two a.m. I'll be awake, fretting with my happy kind of fret.'

'We'll be fine,' Dimity said, suddenly shy.

Lila's eyes softened. 'You will.'

Marcus collected coats. The door clicked shut behind them, and the cottage settled, its sounds returning: the tick, the small sigh of settling timber, and the gentle roar of a fire.

It left behind a deeper quiet.

Vivian turned to her, and the room narrowed to the space they occupied.

'Stay,' Dimity said—not a question, not an apology. 'Stay tonight.'

Something like astonishment crossed his

face, followed by relief so pure she felt it in her own ribs. 'If I do,' he said, voice low, 'it won't be because the cottage wishes it. It will be because I do.'

'Good,' she said. 'Then we agree on what's real.'

His smile was slow, private. He set his glass down, and she did the same. As they crossed the room, the tree lights dimmed a fraction, as if respecting a threshold. The flame in the hearth lowered its bright talk to a murmur. Somewhere upstairs, a floorboard creaked once—familiar, approving.

They climbed the narrow staircase side by side, hands brushing, neither of them rushing. At the landing, Dimity paused and let her palm slide along the smooth banister. How many times had she come up this way alone? How different the house felt now that footsteps matched hers.

At her door, she turned, nerves rising like a tide and then ebbing as she met his eyes. They stood a breath apart. The past week—that cold ache of almost and not yet—tilted and emptied.

'Goodnight,' she whispered, a smile touching the word and changing its meaning entirely.

'Goodnight,' he echoed, understanding the

invitation inside it.

She opened the door. The room held the day's leftover warmth, the bed turned back earlier in hope rather than certainty. The window framed a spill of stars. Vivian stepped over the threshold, and she reached for him.

The rest belonged to quiet. To trust. To the kind of love that overcomes everything that gets in its way.

Outside, the snow fell—small, deliberate flakes crossing the beam of the porch light like moths. Downstairs, the fire burned low, content to be watched by no one. On the mantel, Bea's photograph caught a stray glimmer and let it go.

Just before sleep claimed them, a soft thread of sweet almond drifted and vanished, like a promise that had been fulfilled.

THE END

Subscribe to Annie's newsletter to read when Book 2 of The Enchanted Village is available.

http://annieseaton.net

Also by Annie Seaton

Daughters of the Darling
From Across the Sea
Over the River
By the Billabong
Beneath Still Waters
Under Darling Skies

A Bec Whitfield Mystery
Bowen River
Shadows on the Shore
Storm Season

The Happy Outback Hotel (2026)
Outback Strangers
Outback Secrets
Outback Dreams
Outback Hearts
Outback Spirit
Outback Promise
Outback Horizon
Outback Silence
Outback Whispers
Outback Flame

Duckinwilla Days
Coming Home
Secrets and Surprises
Wishes and Whispers
Chasing Dreams
New Beginnings

ANNIE SEATON

All Together Now

Home to the Outback
Lucy
Angie
Jemima
Isabella

Porter Sisters Series
Kakadu Sunset
Daintree
Diamond Sky
Hidden Valley
Larapinta
Kakadu Dawn

Others
Whitsunday Dawn
Undara
Osprey Reef
East of Alice
One Summer in Tuscany
Four Seasons Short and Sweet
Follow the Sun
Ten Days in Paradise
Deadly Secrets
Adventures in Time
Silver Valley Witch
The Emerald Necklace
A Clever Christmas

A MAGIC CHRISTMAS

Christmas with the Boss
Her Christmas Star
The Emerald Necklace

The Augathella Girls Series
Outback Roads
Outback Sky
Outback Escape
Outback Wind
Outback Dawn
Outback Moonlight
Outback Dust
Outback Hope
Boxed Sets
Augathella Girls 1-4
Augathella Girls 5-8
Augathella Short and Sweet Series
An Augathella Surprise
An Augathella Baby
An Augathella Spring
An Augathella Christmas
An Augathella Wedding
An Augathella Easter
An Augathella Masquerade Ball
Boxed Set
Augathella Short and Sweet 1-3
Augathella Short and Sweet 1-4

Sunshine Coast Series
Waiting for Ana
The Trouble with Jack

ANNIE SEATON

Healing His Heart
Sunshine Coast Boxed Set

The Richards Brothers Series
The Trouble with Paradise
Marry in Haste
Outback Sunrise
Richards Brothers Boxed Set

Bondi Beach Love Series
Beach House
Beach Music
Beach Walk
Beach Dreams
The House on the Hill **Boxed Set**

Second Chance Bay Series
Her Outback Playboy
Her Outback Protector
Her Outback Haven
Her Outback Paradise
The McDougalls of Second Chance Bay Boxed Set

Love Across Time Series
Come Back to Me
Follow Me
Finding Home
The Threads that Bind
Love Across Time 1-4 Boxed Set
Bindarra Creek
Worth the Wait
Full Circle

217

A MAGIC CHRISTMAS

Secrets of River Cottage
A Clever Christmas
A Place to Belong
Hearts in Harmony

Awards

2024: Finalist – Romantic suspense category, RUBY award for From Across the Sea.

2023: Winner - Long contemporary novel category, RUBY award for *Larapinta.*

2023: Finalist - Australian Romance Readers Awards for *Kakadu Dawn,* the sixth and final book in the Porter Sisters series.

2018 and 2020: Finalist - for the NZ KORU Award.

2017: Winner - Author of
the Year, AUSROM.

2016, 2017, 2018, 2019: Longlisted - Sisters in Crime Davitt Awards.

2016: Finalist - Book of the Year, Long Romance, RWA Ruby Awards for *Kakadu Sunset.*

2015: Winner - Best Established Author of the Year, AUSROM.